Superior Sacrifices

Jan Stafford Kellis

Myrno Moss Perspectives

Superior Sacrifices

Jan Stafford Kellis

Myrno Moss Perspectives

This is a work of fiction. The characters in this story do not exist; they were
imagined in whole by the author. Any similarities between the characters in
this story and real people are purely coincidental. Marquette, Michigan and
Madison, Wisconsin, though real, have been modified by the author to fit this
story. The town of Hastings Junction was invented by the author and isn't
patterned after any real towns.

Acknowledgements

This story arrived in my head fully formed one spring day, but it took over a year for it to progress from snippets scrawled in random notebook pages into a readable form. This story is so different from my other books, I ran it by my cadre of editors much earlier in the writing process than usual. After I received positive feedback from them, I proceeded to finish. Thank you, Angie Leonard and Jen Postula, for your enthusiastic responses! You inspired me to finish.

Jean Bloom and Paul Mason also dedicated time they didn't have to help me understand the adoption process; thank you! I hope you both enjoy this story.

Jen Postula deserves one more thank you for brainstorming the title with me; there's no better place to think of a title than in a camper over morning coffee.

Last but certainly not least, I must thank my husband Jason Kellis for putting up with my silences (except for the keys tapping) while I was living with Mitch and Marcia and Daphne, and for helping me design the cover.

Also by Jan Stafford Kellis

FICTION

The Word That You Heard

The Sunshine Room

NONFICTION

Bookworms Anonymous:
A Non-Traditional Book Club For All Readers

A Pocketful of Light:
13 Days in the World's First Tourist Destination

For Jen, my not-quite-twin sister

A great source of calamity lies in regret and anticipation; therefore a person is wise who thinks of the present alone, regardless of the past or future.

-Oliver Goldsmith-

Marcia

It's all I can do to escape the chaos of my home (*my haven? haha*) and the boisterous boys. They're teenagers already, still as busy as toddlers running from one task to the next. No, there's no real haven for a mother except inside her own head, which is where I spend much of my time.

This is the fifth day I've driven to work with no music playing. No inane radio show DJs trying to distract me from the business of life. Just the whoosh of the air as I slice through it, creating an invisible wake of air currents.

This is Zen for me: a breeze providing white noise, a laxative for my imagination. I really should get a tape recorder, or whatever they're called now, to capture the ephemera before it's lost forever.

I like to think of the whoosh as a corridor—maybe

a river between rock walls, capped only by a distant sky—pulling my thoughts out of my head like a magnetic force, powerful and invisible.

By the time I reach the store, I've solved the main character's conflict or invented a side story line with some of the minor characters. Sometimes I envision a book cover and try to create it on the computer; usually I leave the manuscripts coverless, a title page announcing Maggie's latest mystery. Bound with rubber bands.

Evan is tiring of my obsession (his term) and thinks he's being supportive by encouraging me to find an agent. "Your stories are good, Hon," he says in his sunniest voice. "And they might help someone. Just think: if your stories inspire young girls to stand up for themselves and figure things out on their own, you'll make a big difference in their lives!"

"You sound like a commercial."

"I'll be your marketing department!" Evan's voice deepened to his most persuasive tone as he added, "Your books contain a message that deserves to be heard."

Sometime I wish I believed in myself as much as Evan believes in me. Other times I wish no one would notice me at all and I could sail through life on my air current, unencumbered by others' opinions and expectations.

The sign catches my eye as I drive past the store to circle around to the alley parking lot, its paint faded and peeling, and I consider re-painting it to stretch its life another year before investing in a new one. TURN THE PAGE the sign advises, and I realize, not for the first time, I've embraced this philosophy since 1975. Turn the page, forget the past. This never happened. This, too, never happened. Turn the other cheek.

The storeroom beckons me, its funky painted door inviting me inside to behold my manuscripts, neatly stowed in labeled containers, in date order, all 28 of them reposing in the dark without anyone so much as rustling their pages. Patient and content.

I don't remember the last time I was content. Certainly it was before 1975, since I was already a teenager by then, the personification of discontent. I may have been content as a child, after I'd learned to read, before I'd noticed the weight of others' expectations on me.

My unease today is lighter than it was yesterday and lighter yet than the day before. I never know what will trigger another flashback (my term—it feels like a stab in the back, quick as a flash) and so I'm unprepared when one strikes. I believe I will have regained my usual level of placitude (is that a word? the state of being placid?) by tomorrow, which will be the sixth day after being assaulted by Sweet, that old hair band, wailing about the Ballroom Blitz. I don't know why the radio stations won't let that particular substandard rock song die peacefully.

All I wanted to do was hear the news on my way to work. Instead of a dose of current events, I was treated to a brutal anxiety attack. One would think (hope) after 35 years the memory would lose its edge, dulled by countless exposures to the present, and my conscious, logical refutation of the triggering event.

I once read a cross stitch sampler on someone's wall that said: *Eat a live toad first thing in the morning and nothing worse will happen the rest of the day.* I like to think this is true, on a broader scale: Howard was my live toad and nothing worse will happen to me.

Can my history protect my future?

So far, so good.

Evan would say I've allowed my past to paralyze my life and my future. "You need to talk to a professional. It's not healthy for you to only be able to discuss this with me and Mitch." Evan's family is one of those touchy-feely clans, always hugging and kissing hello and good-bye. He doesn't understand the clinical stoicism cultivated in my childhood home, where everyone was always pleasant (not exuberant) or slightly out of sorts (stomach aches were common ailments, to be borne silently and with grace).

"You know I can't discuss it. It never happened," I curl my fingers in the air when I utter those last three words in this, our oft-repeated conversation, because it irritates Evan when people mime quotation marks.

I am a collection of memories and experiences, good and bad, and I can't imagine my life without any one of the events that have so far shaped me. But I still don't like the unease visiting me, however rarely it occurs three and a half decades after the attack, and usually accompanied by the silent, invisible presence of Howard. I say presence (rather than feeling or sense) because he is. Present. He's here.

The science is beyond me, but Howard somehow occupies space for a day or two after I suffer a sharp recollection of Homecoming '75. He creates subtle energies to announce himself (as if I didn't know already before he arrived) such as moving a curtain near a closed window or my least favorite, a shallow breath on my neck. Like a whisper with no words.

Mitch calls this Howard's death breath. Howard seems to spend more time with Mitch and he's matured over the years from spiteful, uppity punk to a helpful, loyal friend. "That's why I think it's all in my head," Mitch says. "Howdy has lost his boyhood personality and somehow aged along with me. Well, the first rule of death is you stop aging."

"What would a psychiatrist say?" I ask, per our standard twin psychoanalyst role play.

Mitch pretends to think for a moment before giving me the stock answer: "You'll have to continue our weekly appointments until I can afford a yacht—I mean, until we can properly diagnose your psychosis."

I would pay to be able to stop analyzing my own psyche.

The front door of my shop opened, jangling the bell and propelling me out of the back room.

"Hey there, Marcia! Beautiful day outside. Got a package here for Mrs. Ainsworth, do you mind?" Troy, the UPS delivery man, plopped a box on the counter. "Sounds hollow. Feels empty," he shrugged, eyeballing the ceiling. "What do you think: dead flies? stale air? broken promises?" He grinned.

"I'll take the package for her, but I think broken

promises weigh a lot more than stale air."

He was already halfway out the door, waving over his shoulder.

Mrs. Ainsworth lives next door to Turn the Page and she's my best customer (besides myself), purchasing a few books each week and minding the store when I have errands to run. She's a retired secretary (her term—these days she'd be called an administrative assistant) and sleeps until 10:00 each morning, which is why her UPS packages are delivered over here.

I'm not sure what my friend roster says about me: aside from my husband and sons, my two closest friends are a profane old woman and a ghost. Shaking my head to clear it, I return to the storage room to regard my manuscripts. I began writing during the long months I lived with Aunt Audrey, mainly to release the words locked in my brain so I could be free to think new thoughts. It was Audrey's idea to fictionalize the story.

"I can't get past the game," I'd told her. "What happened afterward was so bad I want to write it down to let go of it, but it's too hard to write about."

"Hmmm," she cocked her head to one side, wild frizzy hair quivering while she considered. "Maybe you shouldn't write about your own situation *exactly*."

"What do you mean?"

"Well, maybe you should make up a character—um, Maggie or something—and make up things that happen to her. Then it won't be so painful, and you won't be restricted by the truth."

Two weeks later I had completed the first draft of a young adult mystery novel, 21 chapters and nearly 50,000 words long. I spent the rest of that endless winter refining it until it became what I'm holding in my hands today: *Maggie Stands Up.*

The first novel in the series pits our heroine against a ruthless businessman who hires a bodyguard with a sneer to distract Maggie so he can do his vague, nefarious deals. The antagonist is sophomoric at best, but I blame this on my being a sophomore when I created him. Maggie stands up to the body builder, somehow leveraging her weight and toppling him over.

In the end, Maggie exposes the businessman and makes the bodybuilder look like a fool. The last chapter ties right into the next book the same way all subsequent last chapters in the Maggie series do: with Maggie answering the phone and accepting a new assignment.

Throughout her career thus far, Maggie (short for Magnificent—again, I was a sophomore when she was created) Menlo (yes, this reflects my opinion of men at the time) has solved cases involving missing pets, abandoned children and a neglected cabin that yielded clues to the deceased owner's heritage. She's like a tough Nancy Drew.

She's been attacked but never raped.

In the spring of 1980, Mitch and I met Evan in the college cafeteria during a crowded lunch period. We were all finishing our sophomore years, reveling in academia, shocked to realize we were nearly halfway through our college careers.

"Mind if I sit here?" Evan had asked, sliding onto a seat next to Mitch. I couldn't help but notice his blue eyes, set off by an early tan and an impressive set of biceps.

"Sure, no problem. I'm Mitch, and this is my sister Marcia. We were just talking about her test in Biology," he looked at me. "So..."

"Not worth discussing," I said.

"Sounds tough," said Evan. "Did you study?"

"Oh, I'm pretty sure I aced it," I explained. "Hence, nothing to discuss."

He nodded. "I see," he paused. "I'm Evan, by the way."

"Nice to meet you. What's your major?"

"Business management, with a marketing focus. I couldn't decide what to do so I chose something I could do anywhere, even here. What about you? What are your majors?"

"Forensic science."

"Writing."

"You two are both sophomores?" he asked.

"We're twins," we answered together.

Mitch glanced at me. "Did you-"

I shrugged one shoulder in response. "Yeah, if-"

"Oh, that's right."

"And I-"

"Okay. See ya, M." We talked so fast our words almost landed on top of each other.

"10-4, M." Mitch stood, slowing his speech to tell Evan it was nice meeting him, and headed to his next class.

"I'm not normally this nosy," said Evan, "but what did you guys decide just then? What were you talking about?"

"Oh, we are going to the dinner theatre the drama club is putting on tonight. We saw it on the bulletin board earlier this week. I think it's a dollar per ticket, if you want to go."

Evan looked confused. "That was about dinner plans? How in the world—again, I don't mean to pry—but how in the world did you get dinner plans out of that conversation?"

"We each know what the other one is thinking, so of course we each know what the other will say before it's actually said."

"So, you hear words before Mitch speaks?"

"No, it's more of a...a thought transfer. His thoughts or vibes or whatever you want to call them just kind of blast into my brain."

"That's incredible. I wish I knew someone so well I could just say a few words and they'd get whole paragraphs."

I laughed. "It's not always convenient."

"No, I suppose not."

"Well, we were womb-mates and I believe we started communicating a few minutes after conception."

"Hmm. I've never known twins before, or had my own 'womb-mate'," he grinned, "and I find you two fascinating." His eyebrows shot upward on this last word, so I wasn't sure if he was being sarcastic or sincere. "Truly," he said then, "fascinating."

After that we saw Evan more and more often, colliding with him in hallways and encountering him outside the dorm. Mitch confronted him once, needing to ensure Evan wasn't tracking my route, planning to attack me after gaining my trust.

"It's cool," said Evan. "I'm not following your sister. I might ask her out, though, if that's okay with you."

"It's okay with me, but prepare yourself for a lockout," said Mitch. "She hasn't had a boyfriend in a while and she's not shopping yet."

"Okay, well, you can't blame a guy for trying."

And try he did, by carrying my books, offering to accompany me to the library, and acting as a sort of personal assistant or valet. He learned what I liked to eat and started buying my lunch in the cafeteria, waiting at a table near the door to catch me as I walked in.

"What if I'd decided to skip lunch today?" I asked him that first time, eyeing the two lunch trays. He'd grabbed a vase with a tulip in it from a faculty table and placed it on the corner of my tray.

"I guess I'd eat leftover chicken salad sandwich for dinner," he shrugged.

The bell above the door jangles nervously as Mabel Ainsworth strides in, mid-sentence as usual. "-my package? Was The Pipsqueak here?"

"Yes, there's a package for you behind the counter," I chuckled. Mabel refers to most people by some derogatory name; the Napoleon-sized UPS man is usually called The Pipsqueak or His Pips. Mabel tosses herself onto a stool like a loosely organized collection of pick-up sticks, her capris showcasing her bony old lady legs and orthopedic-looking sandals. She clasps and unclasps her hands several times, clicking her rings together on skeletal fingers.

"How are you, dear?" she asks. "You look a bit peaked."

"Oh, I'm fine. I think I just need to sit in the sun."

"Sun can fix a lot," she nods, glancing around.

"How's business?"

I grin at her. "You mean since yesterday? Stellar, of course. I'm working on posters to lure in groups, like book clubs, to offer them a bulk discount when they all become frequent shoppers. What do you think?"

She studies the poster, one finger near her mouth. "I like it, but can you do something about the background? It looks like an old lady's parlor or something."

"Maybe *that's* what's wrong with it," I consider the dusty roses on a beige background. "Yes, I think it needs more funky-ness."

"Yes, funky and hip. You want to attract the hep cats, not the lame ducks."

I met Mabel when I first purchased the building and converted the old meat market into a bookstore, but I first observed her at the cemetery. I'd missed Howard's funeral, scheduled during my third trimester of pregnancy. Thus I'd avoided the awkward decision of whether or not to attend, but I also forfeited the sense of closure the funeral may have afforded me. Upon my return to Hastings Junction I frequently visited Howard's grave and carried on long, silent, one-sided conversations with him. It was a place I could visit when the reality of his final actions and his death, the irretrievable truth of it, weighed me down and invaded my consciousness. The act of addressing him, acknowledging him, seemed to temporarily alleviate my anxiety.

Howard's plot is located in the far corner of the cemetery under a long, leafy maple tree branch just inside the fence. It's peaceful there and the air, when deeply inhaled, invigorates every cell in my body. It's like a deep breathing toxin removal system.

During the visit I'd vowed would be my last (a renewed effort to 'turn the page'), I sat in a lotus position on Howard's site imagining him as an adult. I had graduated college and was planning my wedding to Evan, feeling all grown-up and mature. Howard would have been one of those harried lawyers running from courtroom to courtroom carrying a briefcase everywhere, always the impeccable professional. Victims would have found it easy and comfortable to confide in him. His capacity for persuasion would have fed his family and kept them in high style.

If he'd been able to control his temper, he'd be living large. This was a familiar thought rut, one in which I allowed myself to believe we, Mitch and I, had saved countless others from crippling trauma and deafening shame. That's the hidden cutting edge of the rape victim's unutterable dilemma: society charges the victim with some responsibility for the act, assuming the victim could have halted the attacker, somehow diverted his attention and derailed his violent program, thereby avoiding physical, mental, emotional and psychological damage. (Did some people entertain the notion that the victim was *responsible* for the attack? It seems so, but most sternly chased this thought from their minds without voicing it.)

My thoughts circled in their familiar pattern like a handful of cars on a racetrack. I felt like I was the only person on the planet, with trees, flowers and birds the only witnesses of my life.

"YOU SON OF A BITCH!" My entire body flinched at this intrusion. I focused on a slip of a woman standing about two hundred feet away, ramrod straight, fists clenched at her sides, head tilted slightly down as if she addressed a recalcitrant child. "It wasn't enough that I gave up my dreams for you?" Indignant rage powered her speech. "It wasn't enough that I took care of your sick and sorry ass all those years? I put up with your goddamn drinking, your stupid friends, your laziness and your picky eating and what did you do? What did you do, Henry?" She waited. No answer.

"I'll tell you what you did, you no good rat bastard. You left me here. I'm not forgiving you, Henry," she toned her voice down to a friendly call over a neighbor's fence, talking to someone she couldn't see but nonetheless knew was listening. "Did you hear that, Henry? I don't forgive you," she glanced around the cemetery, apparently still not noticing my car parked behind her in the back corner. "I'm not coming back anymore, either. You're on your own," she trudged over to her car and returned with a professionally wrapped bouquet of roses, tossing it on the grave with the careless attitude of abandoning so much trash.

"This is my last gift to you, Henry. I don't give two shits whether you rest in peace or not. And I won't miss you either, Henry. No Sirree, I sure as hell won't miss you waking me up in the middle of the night to tell me you stabbed your foot opening a can of sardines with your jack knife, or you cut yourself trying to wring out your bottle of Jack Daniel's," she sighed. "Just leave me in peace, Henry. Good-bye." By now she spoke in a slightly loud conversational tone as if compensating for a weak communication signal. She opened her car door and turned back once more to address the grave. "Good-bye, you old son of a bitch," she waved and eased into the car, exiting the cemetery as quietly as she'd entered.

"Well, Howard," I gazed at the clover patch where I imagined his head would be, "you heard her. I'm not forgiving you, I'm not coming back, and you have to leave me in peace." The clover quavered weakly, acknowledging my statement. "Good-bye, you old son of a bitch," I whispered.

The day I bought the store Mabel jogged over from her house to grill me, checking my intentions against her own expectations and finding me tolerable. She showed up again the next morning, paint brush in hand. "You need some help? I know it's like the old saying, lipstick on a whore or whatever it is, but I'd rather sit next to a pretty whore than an ugly one."

"I think the lipstick goes on a pig."

"A pig..." she considered this, looking to her left as if someone stood there. "Well, son of a bitch. I guess we'll decorate a pig, then!" She continued up the walk and let herself in.

After helping me paint all of the interior walls in bold colors and adding quotes about reading in the blank spaces, Mabel appointed herself landscape artist and planted flowers in boxes and set them along the front walk.

"You need an awning," she announced from the sidewalk, arms akimbo, brow furrowed. "A bright one. And a sign up above that hangs from a rod and swings in the breeze." There was apparently no room for negotiation; Mabel had a clear picture of the storefront in her mind and she was prepared to create it accordingly.

Thus she became my decorator, sounding board, muse and mentor. And still I couldn't tell her what kept me up at night. I couldn't explain the fear I felt for Mitch, or Howard's presence (sometimes creepy, sometimes friendly) because I just couldn't bear another human being knowing my whole story. "Once you tell someone something, they can't unhear it. It becomes their burden too, as sure as it's yours, and it becomes a frame through which they view you," Dad had lectured us that ancient autumn, "so you end up bearing the burden twice." He held up one finger, "once in your own mind, your dreams, where it interrupts your sleep and steals your concentration when you're trying to do something, and again," he held up a second finger, "when you see the person in whom you've confided, and they think to themselves, 'there's Mary, the victim' and you lose some of your distinct personality in their eyes because now you have a label and that's how they'll see you forever." Dad, ever the economist, closed the conversation with one of his favorite phrases. "The most economical thing to do in this situation, with the resources at hand, is to tell no one. This will prevent future worries and ensure your burden remains singular."

Over the years, the tight circle of our secret has expanded by one: Evan. When he proposed, I told him yes with one condition: he had to hear something about me and promise never to tell anyone; after that, if he still wanted to marry me, I was ready.

It's dark, living with such a past. It's dark and heavy, like an oaken yoke draped across my shoulders, straining my entire being. And so it's tempting to share, especially with someone like Mabel who is probably brimming with useful advice about how to live with such a past, but Dad's words keep me steady. The last thing I want to do is burden a friend with my past.

I came close once, though. The conversation was innocent enough, a general commiseration about childbirth. I hadn't realized Mabel was a mother until she told me her child had died in a freak accident involving an in-ground pool at a neighborhood kid's birthday party. Engrossed in her story, I absentmindedly mentioned something about the third time I was pregnant and had Owen.

"I thought you only had two kids," she said.

"Oops, I think my closeted skeleton is showing," I studied the far wall briefly, deciding I could share at least part of my secret. "I had a baby in high school and gave it up for adoption."

Mabel's face registered shock, a rare and gratifying sight. "Oh my, Marcia, that must have been terrifying. Both the pregnancy and the adoption."

"Yes, and the delivery was no picnic either."

"Do you know where your first child is? Was it a girl or a boy?" Her cool, papery hand cupped my forearm in comfort.

"It was a girl. Mitch and I always referred to her as Daisy, but I have no idea where she lives or what her name is now." I glanced out the front display window, holding back a sigh. "I don't think of her as often as I probably should; sometimes it seems like a dream, or a story I heard about somebody else. I do wonder, though..."

"Hey Ma, have you seen my tie?" a typical greeting from my younger son.

"Hello, Owen, nice to see you."

"Sorry, Ma. Nice to see you. How was your day? Have you seen my tie?" He hugged me, his shoulder level with the top of my head. The boys' size surprises me every day, my mind's eye stubbornly clutching to their toddler images even as I enjoy their young adult selves.

"Owen, your armpits stink. And please, *please*, close your words. You know how I hate the name 'Ma'."

"Sorry, *Mommmmmm*," he grinned. "Have you seen-"

"Your tie is on your brother," I pointed behind Owen to Simon, strutting through the kitchen and doing a stiff-legged pirouette with his jacket hanging on one finger over his shoulder. Both boys inherited Evan's thick black hair and wide jaw, but they have my deep-set blue eyes.

Owen chased Simon up the stairs to claim his tie (hopefully the tie wouldn't become a noose) while I gulped a cup of coffee and touched up my makeup. We were meeting Evan at the banquet celebrating Mitch's twenty years on the force and his one hundred percent solve rate. His office is full of commendations, medals and letters from grateful victims and prosecutors. He is the most decorated detective in the Iron Falls Police Department, but he dislikes the attention and the public recognition. Solving cases is its own reward, he always says. He takes each case personally, his way of paying something back to society while improving life for others and compensating for his own past.

The boys reappeared, dressed and pressed (or at least less rumpled than usual) and I let Owen drive us to the banquet. "Parking may be a challenge here tonight," I warned him.

"Don't worry, I just learned how to parallel park," he addressed the road while his hands gripped the wheel.

"I don't think Mom wants to subject her precious Tahoe to your pathetic propensity for parallel parking," Simon said. "Preferably, park perpendicularly."

"What wit," Owen gritted his teeth and pulled into the lot, snagging the last available spot.

"Good driving," I complimented him.

"Yes, it was quite the feat, driving in that weather. Oh, wait, there was no weather. I mean driving in the traffic. No, no traffic...hmm. Well, I'm still impressed and thankful that you delivered us all here alive, in one piece so to speak-"

"Enough, Simon! I'm sorry that I got my driver's permit and you don't get to drive as much. Now you know how I felt for the past two years while you drove everywhere. It's my turn. That's just the way it is," said Owen, punching Si in the arm on the way to the door.

"Don't muss or I'll fuss," Simon brushed off his shoulder and stuck out his foot to trip Owen. Owen anticipated Simon's foot and stepped over it, sailing through the door to find our reserved table.

"Simple, simple Simon," muttered Owen.

"It's an open bar," Evan greeted me with a kiss, "so I ordered you a dirty martini."

"What a lovely idea. I knew there was a reason I keep hanging out with you."

"How are the hoodlums?"

"Typical shenanigans. O did a great job driving us here while Si provided commentary."

"I'm glad you're both here," said Evan, nodding at

the boys. "You can fetch our drinks, then drive us both home."

"Sounds sensational," said Simon.

"I'll be the bartender. What would you like?"

"You can't tend bar. You shouldn't even be delivering drinks, but you can probably get away with it since you have connections," Mitch clapped Owen on the shoulder and sat down next to him.

"I'll just say the drinks are for you," Owen grinned. "People will line up to see you tip a few back."

"I bet they would. I'll have one, but that'll be plenty." We all joined in for the chorus, "I have to keep my head on straight." Mitch had never been drunk. He'd kept an unrelenting vigil on his conscious and subconscious since October 18, 1975.

"One of these days, M, you'll have to cut loose with me," I said. I felt his answer: *maybe someday, when we're so old the world won't notice us. We can get drunk and tell tales and everyone will think we're making it all up.*

I nodded and sipped my martini, sharing it with Evan. Owen continued to supply us with martinis, switching to beer when the bar ran out of vodka. Mitch's boss spoke so well of my brother, citing him for solving 34 murders, 16 rape cases and one child abduction, I felt tears welling in my eyes and nearly cried until Evan pressed his hand on my back to steady me.

When I returned to school on the first day of our junior year, it seemed as if I'd never left and no one had noticed I'd been gone. So much for people wondering what had happened to me! Even now, at high school reunions or other casual get togethers with our old classmates, I'll occasionally remark "that must have been the semester I stayed with Aunt Audrey" and no one remembers (or admits remembering) I was missing.

Mitch worked at Greasy Ted's Gas 'N Go every day after school and on Saturdays, so in self defense I found a job at the post office, a coveted position open to me only by virtue of my grade point average and punctuality. I helped sort mail and sometimes filled in for the rural delivery route when old Bernie called in sick, which started happening with some regularity after I was hired and he knew there was someone to cover for him.

Working at the post office was interesting; I

preferred working inside, learning quickly Bernie only called in sick during a snowstorm or rain shower and I'd end up soaked through, delivering damp or dripping packages. In the office, I learned some organizational skills, time management skills and heard all kinds of crazy things through the wall when people came in to retrieve their mail out of the post office boxes. Each voice was distinctive and immediately recognizable to me; I could have won a game of "name that person" in three syllables. Whispered voices, sometimes difficult to identify, meant extra juicy gossip. Most of what I heard was the typical inane small town greetings and inquiries about family members ("How's your mom doing in the old folks' home?" or "Did your dog's leg heal yet?" or "Did you hear about Boomer? He's off the wagon again!").

One day as I sorted a batch of mail which had arrived late during a blizzard, a particular phrase caught my ear.

"—*said* she was staying at her *aunt's*, but I know what *that* is code for!" This had to be nosy old Prissy Perkins, a spinster (this was Gram's term) who had nothing better to do than worry about what everyone else was doing (this was Mom's observation).

"I think I know what you're implying," came the reply, spoken in a confident conversational tone by Lydia Nussbaum, who owned the bookstore in Marquette. "You'd better make sure you're speaking about facts and not supposition. This is a good girl you're talking about, and I won't stand here and listen to you tarnish her reputation."

"But, I'm just *saying*," I could picture old Prissy fluttering her hand up to her chest, "well, she had a pretty flimsy reason for staying at her aunt's for such a *long time*, is all."

"It is none of my business," said Lydia, meaning it was none of Prissy's business, "but to draw so many conclusions from something you heard at the *grocery* store is...well, it's irresponsible of you as an adult in this town. It's shameful, really." I could hear the fury in Lydia's voice. Prissy sputtered an apology as she scuttled out the door.

I could feel my heart beating in my whole body; even my fingertips pulsed. Anxiety locked my lungs. Someone not only believed in me, she defended my character.

I wondered if I deserved it.

I walked across the back yard to Mitch's place, originally intended to house a mother-in-law or maybe servants. He moved in shortly after Evan and I bought our house, announcing he was tired of paying rent to an ungrateful, unrelated landlord and didn't have time to shop for and purchase a house. After Simon was born Mitch helped with childcare whenever his schedule allowed, and over the years the boys enjoyed raiding both refrigerators and seeking their uncle's advice in all life matters, especially those garnering a negative answer from their parents. Having Mitch live so close by has also relieved both of us from learning if we could survive without each other (a thought we never expressed aloud).

Mitch opened the door as my foot hit the top step, his anticipation of my intentions sharpened over time. "Hey," he greeted.

"Hey," I handed him a cup of coffee prepared the

way he preferred, with a half-teaspoon of creamer. He drank it black at work in an effort to simplify, so the addition of cream was his weekend luxury.

"Don't tell me, let me guess," he said, staring into my eyes. "Let's see. You're turning 50 in a couple of weeks and you're taking stock...no, not quite right...you're feeling...weighed down. That's it! You're carrying a burden and it's time to leave it behind. The voices in your head have been repeating themselves and you want to shut them off," his grin softened the truth of his words.

"I like it better when we talk silently. I don't like hearing my thoughts come out of your mouth," I said. "But yes, I think we both need to let Howard die. We've kept him around so long! It's been 35 years, Mitch, and the other day I heard that damn *Ballroom Blitz* song on the car radio and even though I changed the station immediately, I had to pull over just to get through it."

"I know what you mean. That night plays over and over, and sometimes I can't see what's right in front of me because I'm reliving that night and seeing what I saw in 1975," he glanced at the floor. "It's not conducive to clear thinking, that's for sure," he sighed. "And you're right, this is much easier when we do it silently."

I gazed at the one person in the world who

understands me on every level and felt our mutual promise flicker and grow, braiding itself from the past to the future and gathering strength. *It's time to abandon yesterday and focus on the present by trusting the future will be fabulous*, I thought. I felt Mitch agree with me as his squeeze tightened, enveloping me in a healing hug like I hadn't felt since the day I had Owen. I'd always felt that Mitch had made the bigger sacrifice, sticking around while I married Evan and had the boys, living out my happily-ever-after while he worked and purposely avoided long-term relationships.

"How does that go?" he said as he took a step back and picked up his coffee cup, staring at the far wall above my head. "It's time to abandon yesterday's grief and gather strength for tomorrow's hope."

I chuckled. "You made that up."

"Maybe I did, but it's inspiring, just the same," he grinned. "You know, we *have* grieved for Howard. Sincerely and all-encompassingly grieved. If that's not a word, it should be, because that's how we've grieved. And now we can't let the grief kill us. We must be stronger than the grief, and go through it and keep going," he sighed. "I'm about ready to retire. Do you need a stock boy at the store?"

"Um...you just changing the subject, or are you tired of working?"

"I think I'm truly tired of working, at least at this job, and ready to take on something else. Of course, I'm almost fifty, so it could be difficult to find another position. It's just something that's been kicking around the back of my mind."

"Take a vacation. You probably haven't had a day off in...what, ten years? Since we all went to Disney World?"

"I've had a day off here and there, but yeah, no vacation. Maybe I'll put in for some time off and do some projects around here, hang out with the boys, enjoy some free time. Recharge," he paused. "Oh, and I have to attend a seminar in Lansing next week," he shrugged. "In case I don't really retire."

"Lansing? How come they never hold your training programs in the UP?"

"Because Lansing's in the center of the Universe, according to the State."

I knew the moment Mitch died; I felt his heart stop beating. It was the middle of the afternoon and he was 300 miles away. I stumbled and shuffled across the store to flip the sign to *Closed*, all the better to sink to the floor in silent despair. I don't remember driving home. By the time the police who responded to the accident called me, I'd been sitting in stunned grief staring out the window of our sun room at his cottage on the far side of our back yard. I retained only snippets of the conversation: "we regret to inform you..." followed by my hollow, nearly silent "I already know. Please don't say it." But of course they did say it, which made me hold my breath to contain a sudden overflow of impotent, energetic, violent rage. I longed for a shot of whiskey, although I'd never swallowed it straight.

Evan received the same phone call from the same cop and he should have earned a speeding ticket racing home to tuck me in his arms. "You already know," he said when he walked in and saw my face. I think I nodded.

Mitch dying in an automobile accident while on his way to a training seminar was incomprehensible, an incomplete ending. His was a vibrant, exuberant life punctuated by a banal death. I clenched my teeth against the urge to laugh hysterically at the inanity of it all. Then I clenched my fists to stave off the wild crying jag threatening to hold me hostage.

We had always believed we'd grow old together and die at the same time, just as we'd been born. A dual exit. We'd planned this since we learned about death, reasoning our lives would be forever entwined, parallel odysseys that would naturally end as one, but not before we'd attained the age of at least one hundred and one. A number that, when added (1+0+1), equals two.

I didn't speak at the funeral. In fact, I didn't speak at all for a month, plunging into my un-twinned grief. Evan made all of the funeral arrangements, consulting with my parents about details such as appropriate wardrobe and music choices. Mabel ran the store, using her spare key and fortitude to maintain normal operations as closely as possible. Everyone in town knew what had happened, of course, and allowed me my brief departure from society as if my behavior was normal and even expected. Evan and the boys treated me like an invalid (I suppose I was an emotional invalid, though my affliction felt physiological and I have always considered emotional weakness a character flaw). They delivered breakfast in bed, prepared meals and never once asked me when I was going to get dressed or comb my hair.

One day, I woke up and performed my regular morning ritual, showering and dressing (wearing clothes felt both familiar and strange), and headed to the store. Mabel greeted me as if she'd been expecting me; I acted as if she'd always opened the store, and I complimented her on the window display and the new pyramid-shaped arrangement of the staff picks on the table near the door.

It's been one year, sixteen days and three hours since Mitch's death and today I'm boxing up his possessions. This is my fourth attempt at cleaning out his cabin, the previous attempts ending in weak promises to myself to "finish next time". I can't entertain Evan's offers to help, preferring to wallow in solitude.

Difficult as it is to relegate these items Mitch used and loved to my attic, it's easier to smother them in a plastic container than to give them away or donate them to charity. I started with his closet, after Evan removed the clothing (his suits were too much like Mitch imposters, flimsy headless mannequins hanging there ready to spook me, so I broke my own rule and asked for help). The upper shelf supported several boxes, all carefully labeled except one, left blank. I removed everything, setting each container on the bed and verifying the contents (photos, notes from college, notes from seminars, Grandpa's old watch and other trinkets) before finally grabbing the blank box.

The only things inside this box were an old notebook labeled Geography Notes and a few newspaper articles from Mitch's high school football days. I tossed the entire box onto the garbage pile when I realized I'd seen Howard's name in one headline. Reaching for the box again, I examined the contents more closely. The articles were from the months following Howard's disappearance, chronicling his football glory and the recovery of his body. His funeral announcement was included, as well as the graduation ceremony program for that year, which mentioned Howard's name and the legacy he left at Hastings Junction High.

I flipped open the Geography Notes book and recognized Mitch's blocky printing.

There is no statute of limitations on murder. This fact is what prevents me from telling anyone what happened to Howard Barstow on October 18, 1975, so help me god. Not that I believe in god—it's just an expression, like 'can you dig it' or 'holy wah'. I know a murder committed in self defense or even in defense of a weaker person is justifiable, but the murderer is still labeled and what are the odds a judge would believe my sister didn't lead him on?

I'd known, of course I'd known, what (who) had happened to Howard. I knew it in my bones, through the usual method of thought transference I shared with Mitch.   Learning he'd coped with his heinous act by recording events in writing left me shocked and momentarily deaf and dumb, disbelieving my eyes and unable to trust what I could plainly see in my hands.

I read on.

When people are drunk personalities are warped, sometimes beyond recognition. Any judge could easily blame Marcia for enticing Howdy, teasing him into a state of adolescent arousal so powerful he didn't realize she'd switched from happy curiosity to terror in a matter of seconds. I'd be tried as an adult and tucked away tidily for the next twenty-five years. Unless I got the death penalty. There's a thought that sends a shiver through a fellow. I've watched enough Ellery Queen and Rockford Files to know if I tell anyone anything, I'll get caught. It would just be a matter of time.

Mr. Mattson just taught us about the statute of limitations, which I found very interesting, until he said it doesn't apply to murder. He said there are many forms of evidence the police can use to catch a criminal. Only he called it a perpetrator, probably so he could sound more like Jim Rockford. We've been learning more and more about the criminal justice system since Howard disappeared even though the police don't yet 'suspect foul play'.

I remembered those first few days after Howard's disappearance;   Mitch was so nervous I'd started calling him Twitch. I had yet to learn I carried Howard's child.

I think Mr. Mattson might have been happier if he'd been a detective instead of a high school teacher. Then he could go around saying things like "this perpetrator definitely did not exhibit an attention to detail" or "Aha! What have we here? A shred of fabric that matches the perpetrator's Sunday best jacket." He would have been in his glory.

The police interviewed me. I wasn't their number one suspect or anything, but I was Howard's friend and one of the last people to see him and they interviewed everyone who was at the hunting camp that night. Marcia said she left the camp before Howdy did because she felt sick and the cops believed her. I had to answer their whole list of questions, but that's okay because I'm sure they won't find anything. And I lead the search, calling his parents to report his car was parked down the road to the camp with the driver's door gaping open and no sign of Howard anywhere.

It was hard not to laugh at the beginning of the interview because I was so keyed up my stomach was flipping and twisting about, and the first few questions were about my name and address and how I know Howard, and the policemen already know the answers to those questions because they live in the next town over and they always patrol Hastings Junction. They practically watched me and Howdy grow up, and suddenly they want to know when we met and how well we know each other.

After I clamped down on my hysteria and it was clear I wouldn't let out a squeaky giggle or anything equally incriminating, I was able to more calmly answer the remaining questions about when I last saw him (around eleven o'clock) and what state I thought he was in (drunk, happy) and where I thought he was going (to the store or his house, maybe to get something to eat or a change of clothes). When I asked if I could continue searching they said I couldn't physically search because they didn't want me to find my friend in a 'bad circumstance' but any information I could give them about where to search would be taken into advisement.

Although I assumed they would begin at Howard's car and track him from there, I suggested several other places he might be hiding out, like Bard Lake or the Flats.

And that's how I attempted to control the search. They never checked Bicycle Swamp.

***

I'm so nervous I can barely function. I've only eaten crackers for the past three days and Mom thinks I have the flu. She calls me sixteen times from work every day while I lie here on the couch staring at the wall. I asked her not to call so often because I'm tired of dragging myself to the phone in the kitchen sixteen times per day but she says she needs to know I haven't disappeared.

***

I went back to school after taking a week to recuperate. Everyone says I'm still pale and they blame it on the flu, keeping their distance and crossing their index fingers to ward off my germs. Mrs. Pendergast thinks I got sick because I searched so long and hard for Howard and let myself catch a chill.

My guts don't know whether to feel empty or guilty or if they should keep twisting and flipping, so they just feel tense and blank and slightly nauseous. This must be like what they call shell shock, like soldiers get in wars. I feel like nothing will surprise me enough to cause a reaction. Nothing will warm me enough to completely get rid of this low-level chill in my bones. Nothing will allow me to fully relax into a deep, comforting sleep.

***

We had an assembly at school today. It wasn't a pep assembly, it was a sad and strange assembly. The police were there, and Howard's parents, and they asked everyone

61

in the student body to come forward with any information about Howard, even if we think it won't help the case, because they're getting desperate.

I'd forgotten about that assembly. Mitch's observations brought it back in full color, making me feel as if I could see the whole event as I floated somewhere near the ceiling in the back corner of the gym.

My cell phone chimed, jarring me back to reality with a message on the screen reminding me to prepare my wholesale order for next week's new arrivals. I stashed the notebook and worked quickly to pack up the remaining items. The quiet was short-lived.

"Hiya, Mom," Owen hurtled through the screen door and skidded to a stop in the kitchen. "I keep forgetting this thing is empty," he said, shutting the refrigerator door.

"Take this box to the attic and I'll make a fabulous dinner," I offered. Since Mitch's death I'd neglected the boys, unable to spare any energy for anything other than piloting myself around. Finding Mitch's notebook was like hearing his voice again, and having him hover over my shoulder while I read.

"Deal!" Owen grabbed the box and jogged back to the house, eager to feed his ever expanding appetite.

My next opportunity to read didn't present itself until the following day in the store.

Howard's been missing for a week and they have no leads.

So the police chief said, "I am speaking to each one of you; I implore you to hear me on an individual basis." We all looked around at each other, wondering what the heck he meant. He continued, "I know everyone in this room knew Howard. Ah, I mean, *knows* Howard. We are prepared to take information without repercussion at this point. What this means to you is, if you know something about Howard's whereabouts and you tell us what you know, we will not hold you responsible for any criminal acts that may or may not have occurred. This is your free pass, folks. Howard's parents just want him back safe and sound and they are not interested in pressing charges."

No one moved. The bleachers at Hastings Junction High have got to be the most uncomfortable slabs of wood on the planet and usually people are squirming about, seeking any small comfort they can, but during the strange and sad assembly no one moved. I'm not sure if anyone even breathed. It didn't take long for the police chief to give up; he'd been gauging the audience the entire time he spoke, making eye contact with every person in the room, and apparently didn't detect anything out of the ordinary.

Howard's parents spoke next, saying how proud they are of Howard and how they're certain he's still alive and they expect him to walk through the door at home any minute, but if anyone here sees or hears anything to please, please, *please* call them any time of day or night and we don't have to leave our names. It's not like they wouldn't recognize the voice anyway, especially if the person calling said three or more words.

After the Barstows left the gym, Mrs. Fletcher asked the police chief what will happen next. Everyone straightened their backs and leaned forward, suddenly intent on what he was going to say. "We've already passed the time frame for a missing person case. Right now, that's what this is: a missing person case with no foul play suspected. We are still in search mode and we have issued an APB with Howard's picture on it to all police stations across the country. Someone, somewhere, has to have seen this boy. It's just a matter of getting his picture out there so he's recognized."

I wondered if they'd get a call from a rogue wolf or coyote alerting them to Howard's whereabouts, but they probably didn't hang any posters in the swamp.

My last glimpse of Howard flickered briefly through my mind: mud clinging to his face, dead grasses and reeds plastered to his head, an open gash on his left arm. I shivered, wondering if the smell of his blood had lured a hungry animal.

I suddenly realized everyone was standing up, walking down the bleachers to their next class, so I mingled with the crowd and flowed out the door past the policemen.

***

I've decided to keep writing in this notebook. I have to tell someone these things and there's no one to tell. Marcia probably knows but we can't discuss it. If I write everything down that I can't say out loud, maybe it will eventually evacuate my head and leave me in peace. It's dangerous to put these things in writing but I will just make sure it stays hidden in the false bottom in my desk drawer. This notebook is like a doctor. A shrink. I can tell it everything on my mind and it won't tell a soul, as long as I keep it in its hiding place. Also, I'm labeling the front cover 'Geography Notes' so no one will want to open it if they do find it.

Mrs. Fletcher would be proud of me for writing such a long report. This is much longer than the papers I usually turn in to her, but I guess it's not really fair to compare this to an essay about *The Scarlet Letter* or *The Tell-Tale Heart*. This is a report, though, more than it is a journal or diary. I'm reporting on the events and the causes and effects of the events of one Homecoming Night in Hastings Junction in Michigan's Upper Peninsula.

I wonder what detectives are allowed to write in their

reports when they work on cases. I guess they can only write down the facts and things they observe, but they probably can't write down their ideas about what happened or who did it. Not in the official report, anyway. I think that would be unprofessional and it probably wouldn't stand up in court.

So they probably can't write about how scared the perpetrator is, or how his stomach insists on twisting and flipping and he continues to have trouble breathing evenly and behaving normally.

***

I snuck over to the Barstows' house last Wednesday when I knew they were both working and painted their porch. I remembered Howard grumbling about it, saying now the yard work was finished his dad wanted a fresh coat of paint on the porch. "Most people would wait until spring, but not my folks," he'd said. "Who wants fresh paint under the ice and snow?" he shook his head. "It'll look nice for Halloween," I'd told him, and this is what I thought as I painted the white lattice and dark brown porch floor, envisioning the Barstows' surprise upon their return home from work that day.

I hung a sign on the post that said CAUTION! WET PAINT and hoped they didn't think Howard had snuck out of whatever woods they supposed he was camping in to paint their porch like the good son he was.

I feel better and worse for painting the porch.

To think I'd almost tossed this notebook in the trash! Mitch's most intimate thoughts on his most regretful act had almost become landfill. I visualized it lying on a heap of trash, its cover blowing open, inviting someone to read these passages.

For the first time since our marriage, I withheld information from Evan: I didn't breathe a word about the notebook, guarding it possessively, carrying it everywhere tucked in my large tote bag between store receipts and wholesale catalogs.

Reading it became my guilty pleasure, my secret companion (invisible friend?) accompanying my morning coffee before Mabel came over to reel me back in and make me face the drudgery of daily realities.

One thing that took the spotlight off Howdy's disappearance, at least for a couple weeks, was the Edmund Fitzgerald. Howard disappeared on October 18 (I will never forget that date as long as I live) and the Fitzgerald went down in a horrendous storm on November 10. All twenty-nine crew members were lost to Lake Superior and the news channel put Nixon in the back seat and focused on the freighter's fatal sinking and everyone, from teachers to preachers to cops to criminals, grieved and mourned whether they knew those men or not. Hastings Junction hadn't recovered from Howard's loss yet, most people still hoping or believing he'd stroll down main street and say he'd just had a wild hair to take off but now he wanted to come home, and the Fitzgerald wreck stole some of Howard's thunder. Not that anyone forgot about Howard, but no one knew yet if he'd come home unharmed and we already knew the fate of those twenty-nine lost men.

I've been driving a lot, the car wandering just like my

mind, turning aimlessly from back road to back road. We aren't sixteen yet and don't have driver's licenses, but Mr. Gouth, the town constable, told Dad that as long as Marcia and I aren't hot rodding around and we observe all traffic laws such as using our blinkers before turning and stopping when we see a school bus with a red flashing light, he'll let us drive. Actually, he said more kids should drive more miles because practice is what makes a good driver great.

After the Fitzgerald went down I found myself driving to Paradise a couple times, just to walk the beach and look out at cold, frigid Mother Superior, as we call the lake around here.

Swallowing twenty-nine men hasn't changed the lake one bit. I hope I still look the same to everyone else, but at the same time I hope I don't.

What kind of person can kill another person without any noticeable change in their appearance?

***

Conversation in Hastings Junction usually centers around the weather. I think it's because we already know what's going on with everyone's life, who is going on vacation, who just got back, who has a clean house, who keeps a shrine to their deceased husband on the mantel, and so when we meet each other in public we need something to talk about. If we talked about our personal lives, every other sentence would be, "Yes, I heard that," or, "Yes, I know about that." The weather, boring as it is, provides a subject everyone can talk about and no one knows what will happen. It changes every fifteen minutes or so, from hot to cold or windy to still, so a guy could sit in one spot all day long and talk to every single person about the weather and never have the same conversation twice.

Anyway, after the Edmund Fitzgerald went down, people stopped talking about the weather for a month or so and instead asked, "Where were you when the Fitz went down?" or "What were you doing when you heard about the wreck?" or "Did you know any of the twenty-nine lost souls?" I don't know why everyone said lost souls instead of lost men.   Dad said the media kept calling the sailors souls because it sounded sadder, but I thought losing men sounded sadder because men are physical human beings. Anyway, it didn't matter if the wind was blowing the November rain sideways, people would stop long enough to share their Fitzgerald experiences.

We had the strangest Thanksgiving dinner ever. Marcia knows she's in trouble and she won't tell anyone but me. Technically, she didn't tell me either, but I figured it out. She was so tense during dinner she didn't hear half the conversation and even Grandma Effie tapped her on the shoulder and said, "Excuse me, dear? Can you please return to this table now and participate in our discussion?" and Marcia nearly jumped out of her skin, going three shades paler than usual and I knew she was going to be sick. After she left the table I explained to everyone that she hadn't felt well all day and the flu bug or whatever it was had finally caught up to her. After that the dinner was closer to normal, except Marcia was in her room lying down instead of sitting next to me at the table.

I remembered that Thanksgiving dinner, too, as if I could view it on TV. It was black and white in my mind (the color must have faded with age) but the picture was clear and the sound crisp. My nausea visited me daily then, with no regard for the clock. Morning sickness, with all three of my pregnancies, occurred throughout the day and night.

Mitch's latest communication with me, as I've come to regard this notebook, is at once heartrending and illuminating. It feels like he's blowing the dust off my memories, exposing them in all their fragility to light and air, challenging their integrity.

"-this day? It's absolutely gorgeous outside!" Mabel strode through the door, the jangling bell swallowing her words, and clattered onto her favorite stool across the counter from me.

"What? It's nice out? I don't think I've looked

74

outside all morning!" I grinned at her, but I could feel the fakeness emanating from my face and eyes, the utter futility of trying to project a positive countenance.

"No shit. One look and I can tell you haven't seen the sun in many moons," she clicked her rings together. "Got any coffee made? What's an old dame gotta do to get a good cuppa joe around here?"

"Well, if I see an old dame, I'll ask her. Here you go," I slid the hot mug across the counter.

She held the cup in both bony hands and studied me out of the corner of her eye. "How are you holding up, Marsh? I mean, truly, how are you doing?"

I stared out the window for a long beat before answering, feeling Mitch's gravity in my legs and feet, as if my grief had gained weight and somehow pooled there, an invisible anchor. His presence used to feel so light, like a gossamer tether, and now it was like two gallons of some viscous substance (paint? blood? honey?) rendering my limbs heavy and unwieldy. Mabel waited for my answer. "Truthfully," I began, suddenly needing to fill my lungs with air, "It feels like I'm carrying Mitch around inside myself now instead of being joined to him by invisible threads. It sounds wacky, I know, but I feel so much heavier now, even after I've lost fifteen pounds-"

"I've been meaning to talk to you about that, too. You're too damn skinny."

"Thanks, but I'm almost back down to pre-college weight, so I'm still within the safety zone," I took a sip of coffee. "I don't know what this is like; it's impossible for me to explain it, and I don't know if it's like losing a spouse or child or what you'd compare it to. It just feels like I lost part of myself, but at the same time I have more to carry everywhere I go. Mitch and I are constantly conversing in my head now, too. It's not quite the same as when we would talk silently, when he was alive, because now sometimes I catch myself wondering 'what would Mitch say next?' and of course before, I always received what he was saying."

"It sounds a lot like losing a spouse to me. Not," she held up one finger, "that the loss of my SOB can in any way compare to your loss. But, I have friends who have lost perfectly nice, respectful husbands who describe it sort of like you are." She hopped up then, suddenly intent on dusting the books shelved near the back of the store. *Even SOBs are grieved,* I thought.

My next opportunity to read Mitch's words came three days later.

I feel like I'm viewing my life through a window, reality masked by a fogged pane of glass that makes it difficult to see and hear what's really happening. The Bionic Woman is Marcia's heroine and every time we watch it, I can feel Marcia wishing the story was true and that she could be that bionic lady on the screen, strong and sure and healthy.

She's not sick every day now, but she feels like she's just getting over the flu only it never goes away completely. It's hard for her to concentrate in school and she dropped cheerleading, saying she twisted her ankle and couldn't jump for a while.

Marcia wanted to wait until after New Year's to tell Mom and Dad about her predicament, but she said it's too hard to keep it inside any longer. "Besides," she said, "what if I wait too long and they wish they'd had more time to figure out what to do?" We stared at each other for a minute and a half and she spoke my thoughts aloud: "What if they don't know what to do? I'll be so ashamed if everyone finds out about this."

Of course I assured her no one will find out, but we

both know we live in the gossipingest place in the world. Everyone knows about Prissy Perkins's dad, old Pickle Perkins, who liked to entertain certain gentlemen with his shades drawn after Prissy's mom died. And everyone knows Bob Wychowski married Susie Waterford seven months before she had a baby even though it wasn't Bob's, and he raised little Christopher as his own. Everyone even knows where the key to the Constable's office is kept because one time he locked himself out and tried to get in through a window, but got stuck halfway and had to be rescued by the fire department. That's when the Hastings Junction Fitness Focus started, but it only lasted for about three months.

No one could find out about Marcia. If even one person found out, she'd share the same status as the others, her private business a matter of fact among our friends and neighbors, and everyone acting like nothing was out of the ordinary. Until she left the room, when the busybodies would begin their righteous tattling. "You know," I can picture them saying, snooty and haughty and condescending, "she's the one who had a baby in high school. I wonder if she knows where it is now. It nearly ruined her life, but now she acts like she's Miss Innocence. She's been around the block, that one." I couldn't bear it if people talked about Marcia that way.

Oh, they'd be quick to pass judgment on Mom and Dad and even Grandma Effie and Gramps. I can just hear them saying it's no wonder Marcia got into such trouble, and wouldn't Gramps just roll over in his grave. People have no business assuming they know everything about someone else's business. "There's always part of the picture you don't know," Gramps used to tell me. "Some detail or circumstance, pertinent at the time to the person who made the choices, that we can't begin to understand. It's best not to get drawn into the gossip talk." The tough part is, it's so easy to get drawn into it! Especially in this town.

Marcia would be labeled for life if word of this pregnancy got out.

***

Today was the day. Marcia finally buckled and told Mom and Dad everything.

After dinner I went to get Marcia, to stand by her while she told our parents about her encounter with Howard Barstow the night of his disappearance and hope they didn't draw any homicidal conclusions.

Marcia looked green. I couldn't tell if it was the baby making her so sick, or the thought of telling Mom and Dad, or both. When her eyes met mine I saw it was more because of Mom and Dad so I held her hand like we used to do when we were little kids and old ladies would ask our mom, "How cute! Are they twins?" and we'd sing out, "Our name is Mitchandmarcia and we are pleased to meet you!"

Tears rolled down my face and plopped on the page, rudely injecting present-day awareness into my reverie. I suddenly felt the need to capitulate, to deny my stoic heritage and cry and scream and rage, lament with the ululations of the ancient peoples so the world could hear and feel my loss. Why didn't anyone understand that while I still walked and talked, I was dead as sure as Mitch and Howard? How can a half be the same as a whole? The unjust reality crashed around me, spinning the room and turning my focus inward and backward to 1975 and back from there, back to our childhood and our best memories, where it seemed the sun always shone and our smiles never shut off.

Helpless to abandon the notebook, I read on through my tears. Sometimes I thought Mitch came and sat next to me, hovering over my shoulder to view his words, but mostly I realized I sat alone, my right side feeling oddly exposed and slightly chilled where he should have been.

She gripped my hand and let me guide her to the living room, where Dad stood at the TV cranking the dial through all five channels, searching for something other than Nixon or Fitzgerald. Mom came in drying her hands on a dish towel, wondering aloud what we had to tell her that couldn't possibly wait until she'd finished the dishes.

Marcia and I stood and invited our parents to sit on the couch, the better to absorb our news. I communicated to Marcia through our hands, letting her know I wouldn't leave her alone to face anything, ever, and urging her to begin talking, to get the shock out in the open so it would lose some of its power.

"Marcia has something to tell you. It's pretty heavy, so please don't interrupt until she finishes." Mom and Dad nodded like robots, searching first my face then Marcia's, then studying the wall behind us as they waited in agony for her to begin.

"It's about Homecoming Night," Marcia squeaked, then cleared her throat, "Homecoming Night and the... events that happened after the game."

"Is this about Howard's disappearance?" asked Mom. Dad shushed her and gestured for Marcia to continue.

"Take your time, honey," Dad whispered.

Marcia drew a huge breath and let it out so slowly I think she may have stopped time for a few seconds. "It is about Howard, but it's about what happened before he disappeared. You know we were at a party at his dad's hunting camp," our parents nodded again; I noticed they were now clutching each other's hands, mimicking Marcia's and my grasp. "Well, he drank more beers than he probably should have, and he started getting...friendly with me. I mean, friendlier than usual." Mom sucked her breath in quick but didn't say anything, so Marcia continued, "Before I knew what he had in mind, he threw me on the bed in the back room and pinned me down and...and I told him no, I really did, I told him no over and over again, but he didn't listen and...well, you know."

"After that, he disappeared. I found Marcia just as Howard ran out the back door," I filled in. Now Mom looked as if *she* suffered from morning sickness. Dad just looked furious.

"I didn't say anything before because it didn't seem like as big a deal as Howard running away," said Marcia, gathering volume and speed, "and I didn't want his parents to find out in case he'd get in trouble, and I figured he'd be in enough trouble just from running away, but now I have to say something because I'm...well, I'm in the family way and I'm scared to death and I don't know what to do." She stared at the floor, afraid to raise her eyes to our parents' faces. My ears rang.

"That's it, you can talk now," I finally ended the silence when the tick of the clock, normally undetectable, prevented me from forming a useful thought. I swallowed hard to push the lump back down out of my throat.

"Who knows about this?" asked Dad.

"Only the people in this room," said Marcia.

After five minutes had stretched to feel like a week and a half, Dad held an impromptu family meeting and instructed Mom, Marcia and me to never, ever breathe a word of this to anyone. This order included discussing 'the situation', as he termed it, within our own house. "After tonight," he said, "we won't mention this again unless it's absolutely necessary, and even then, we'll simply call it 'the situation'. The only way to keep a secret in this town is to lock it up and leave it behind—don't think about it, don't act on it, don't talk about it. Just get your heads around it right now so you can leave it behind and move on. I'll figure out how to handle this and I'll let you know what the plan is. After that..." he zipped his lip and threw away the key as we all nodded, mimicking his actions.

While this sounded like a good rule to have in place, it never happened. We discussed the situation constantly, tirelessly running what-if scenarios, lamentations, statements of regret. We didn't talk to Dad about it very often because when the subject surfaced it felt like we were breaking his rules, but the conversation between us and Mom lasted for weeks. Mom and I still mention it sometimes, when we see a young pregnant girl or on the anniversary of Daisy's birth, a conversational snippet here and there so each knows the other hasn't forgotten.

"I have something to say before we have to stop talking about it," said Mom.

"Of course," said Dad, inviting her to talk.

"Marcia, you didn't do anything wrong here. You're not in trouble, from us anyway, and I don't want you to think this was your fault." I knew tears were filling Marcia's eyes. Her fingers gripped mine so hard I thought she'd break my hand. "Sometimes boys are aggressive, and it's not right. Sometimes it's like they lose their minds or something." She looked at me as she finished her short speech and I wondered if she detected any aggression in my face.

***

Dad announced his plan on Christmas Eve, three days after Marcia's confession: to let Marcia finish out this semester in January and then send her to live with Mom's sister Aunt Audrey so she can have the baby and give it up for adoption and no one will find out. He ran the numbers, of course, as he does with every heavy decision, and determined this course of action presents the least chance of detection and the greatest chance of preserving Marcia's reputation and continuing our quiet, drama-free existence here in the gossip center of the north. Abortion was mentioned once but Mom put the kibosh on that option right away because she said someday Marcia might want to have a baby on purpose and she doesn't want to take the chance of something going awry. She's always worried about something going awry. I think she's terrified of things going awry.

Aunt Audrey is pretty cool— she always wears funky clothes and chunky shoes with tall heels and red lipstick. She works in a law office in Madison, Wisconsin, about a five hour drive from here. Maybe four hours if you're in a hurry and scared because your daughter is going to have a baby at the ripe old age of sixteen, which is what Mom kept repeating that first week after Marcia told them.

I don't know how I'll survive for six months without Marcia. We've never been apart for longer than one night.

***

Christmas day arrived in a gloomy fog perfectly matching my mood. The four of us sat around staring at the tree, relaxing until Grandma Effie came over and forced us to act like properly excited Christmas celebrators. Smiles were wooden; thank yous were thin and lifeless. Even the lights on the tree seemed dim.

"It's only six months," Marcia said, glancing at each of us that evening. The four of us were in the living room drinking hot chocolate and playing Clue on the coffee table, Mom and Dad distracted and gray. Marcia's relief in sharing her burden showed on her face and in her posture, like she was no longer weighted down by an unknown future.

"Marcia's right," Mom took a deep breath. "Before we know it, this incident will be over and the situation will be behind us. Next year at this time we'll be saying 'I can't believe Marcia lived with Aunt Audrey for six months'…"

"And helped her recover from surgery," the four of us finished in unison. It felt good to be silly for a minute and sneak a laugh in before my dinner threatened to come flying back out.

"Mitch, I know you are the murderer," said Dad in a mock serious tone.

"What?" I whispered, feeling suddenly faint. The room took on a distressing shade of red and tilted slightly. I could no longer hear anything beyond the ocean roaring in my ears.

Dad said something else and laughed, reaching for the envelope to see if his theory was correct. He slowly withdrew the tiny rope and the cards showing Colonel Mustard and the Library. I finally realized he'd been accusing my game piece of murder: I was Colonel Mustard. And Dad had solved the crime.

Now it was my turn to take a deep breath.

***

Marcia and I spent New Year's Eve watching Dick Clark on TV and eating popcorn. It was by far the best New Year's Eve ever. Mom and Dad were at a party at the town hall, boogying down to their old folks' music and drinking spiked punch. They staggered home around three in the morning, long after Marcia and I were in bed.

She's tired and hungry, and feels awful most mornings. I keep some saltine crackers in my locker at school in case she needs them to settle her stomach and so no one will notice that she's sick in the mornings and keeping crackers at hand. That's all we need, for someone to put those two details together along with Howdy's disappearance.

It's a good thing Jim Rockford isn't on this case.

With the biologically uncontrollable egocentricity of teenage hormones, I always viewed the whole situation as my own: my body, my fault, my sacrifice. I'd considered the effects of my actions on the baby (Daisy?), but never really on my parents.   Now it seems cruel of me to prevent   my parents from knowing their own granddaughter;   I wonder if they ever felt cheated. Watching them with my boys from the moment they landed on Earth, it was obvious my parents were born to be grandparents. They both enjoyed spending time with the boys, teaching them things and traveling with them. Simon is both chauffer and bag boy for my mom when she goes shopping, and Owen is my dad's gardening protégé. Dad discovered the economy of seeds about ten years ago and now cultivates an impressive vegetable garden, each summer's plantings designed to provide most of their vegetables for the year.

I wonder if Daisy has grandparents. Does she have

two sets? I hope she hasn't wanted for anything; I fear she's felt rejected or unloved, if she was told of her own adoption. Suzie, the woman at the adoption agency, assured me she'd handpicked Daisy's new parents, and they were financially comfortable, down-to-earth people who believed in hard work and family. They were just unable to conceive, which seems supremely unfair when one considers they adopted a baby born to someone who was an unwilling participant in the conception.

I remember the minute Howdy stopped struggling. My hands were around his neck, squeezing, shaking him back and forth, my whole body involved in the motion. I was staring at my hands, wondering if they were really mine, and then I noticed his eyes were bulging out and his face was contorted into a primal scream but all he emitted was a weak whispery cry, sounding like the wind blowing through dead cattails. My hands squeezed ever harder, clamped around his neck, and I had a moment of sudden clarity. I think they call this an epiphany, but I'm not sure if it qualifies as something so official and life changing; it felt like I had figured something out and I knew it to be true in my bones. I was that certain of its truth and power. I flashed back on our friendship as if I held a deck of pictures in my hand and could flick through them, catching glimpses of Howard grinning, laughing, running away, climbing trees, suited up for football. And this was the inglorious end of Howard Barstow. He was supposed to become a lawyer. He'd always answered the question, "why do you want to become a lawyer?" with: "So I can sue the pants off people; why else?" Then he'd grin his signature grin, kind of a shit eating, smart ass smile not unlike the Joker in the Batman comics and laugh until everyone present laughed along with him.

Whenever I think of Howard, he's grinning that insane grin.

***

The winters are long and torturous here, but most people don't seem to notice. We all just plug along, bundling up in coats, hats, scarves and boots every time we stick our noses outside. February and March are usually the two longest months, even though February is the shortest. Gramps used to say we are victims of the weather, and these are the two months we are reminded of that daily. It's only January, but I'm dreading it already.

Howard and I used to hang out in the winter when we had no other activities going on. We'd go sledding down Boom Boom Hill or go ice skating on Weavers' pond or if we could get a ride we'd walk along Lake Superior and check out the ice caves.

One time, Howdy and I were sledding, resting at the bottom of the hill before dragging ourselves and our sleds back to the top when he said, "You know Bicycle Swamp?"

"Yeah," I'd replied, thinking of the small swamp located near his dad's hunting camp. It had no official name but everyone called it Bicycle Swamp because someone had tossed a bicycle in it one time and it disappeared with a big *bloop!* sound and was never seen again. It was like the swamp swallowed it and belched out a thank you.

"My dad was just saying last night he wouldn't be surprised if there are bodies buried in there. Oh, it's small for a swamp," he watched my expression, switching from bland interest to doubt, eager for me to believe his dad's theory, "but it's almost like quicksand. It's like quick-mud, super deep and ever hungry for anything someone chucks into it. If we had the Mafia around here, I bet they'd buy that swamp right away and build a ramp right to the middle of it."

"Yeah, they could just back up and dump out the bodies," I said, standing up to collect my sled and begin my ascent.

"Anyway, it just got me thinking," Howard rattled on, "I wish there was a way to drag the bottom, if there is a bottom, or get an excavator or something and just start digging and see what we find. Don't you think that'd be cool? Maybe we'd find a car with a whole family in it or something!"

"You're weird, Howard," I finally said, hoping to steer him to a topic of conversation closer to normal. "Maybe you should become an archeologist. Then you could dig up dead people and get paid for it."

"Holy wah, that'd be so cool. But no, I'm going to be a lawyer, remember?" He laughed, "You never know, you might need a lawyer to do you a favor someday."

"Race you to the top of the hill," I took off like Fred Flintstone, running in place in the slippery snow for a minute before my boots caught and propelled me forward.

Did my subconscious remember the Bicycle Swamp idea at the critical moment when I knew I'd need a place to put Howard? It's dotted with tag alders and cattails, making it nearly impossible to tell if someone has walked through it. My shoes and clothes were already muddy just from walking around Howard's dad's hunting camp property; I'd slipped and fallen in the mud when I got out of the car and everyone had noticed the big swath of mud going up my right side. Later on I realized it was a lucky fall: it provided me with an explanation for the mud on my clothes.

If the card catalog in my mind retained information about how to dispose of a body does that make me a homicidal maniac?

I stare in the mirror sometimes, looking for madness like it's a rash or bruise, easily detected by a casual observer. My eyes don't have the nutcase glint Charles Manson's have, and I don't feel any different inside, but I worry. Is this something I have to control now? Like alcoholism or a speech impediment? I know a guy who only stutters when he's drunk and it gives him away even if he can still walk a straight line. What will give me away? Can others see the crazy glint in my eyes, invisible to me?

Will I ever be able to grieve honestly for my friend?

The victims keep presenting themselves, I thought. I'd never considered Mitch a victim, but he, my parents, Aunt Audrey, Daisy, and even Evan and the boys are all victims of this sorry string of events. Howard's parents, his other relatives and friends, teachers and girlfriends (I'd known he usually pledged his loyalty to more than one at a time) are victims. One could even go so far as to say his future friends, girlfriends and wives, and children, never to be born now, are victims.

"What's for dinner?" Owen came sailing into the kitchen, Simon on his heels.

"Hey, boys!" I smiled gamely, telling myself I looked perfectly focused on the present, "I'm making venison stew. It's the last of the venison from last year, and it'll be ready in about forty-five minutes."

"Smells splendid," said Simon.

"Where's dad?" asked Owen.

"He's working late, meeting with clients in

Marquette.   Well, hopefully they'll be clients.   He's presenting an estimate to them right now."   I stirred the stew and ground some fresh pepper into it.   "We aren't waiting dinner for him, so don't worry about that."

"Oh, good! I'm starving," said Owen.

"Presenting the Prince of Perpetual Pangs," said Simon. Owen and I groaned and rolled our eyes.

The banter continued while I observed as objectively as possible and wondered how Si and Owen would react to learning they have a half-sister someplace in the world. Is Daisy as witty as the boys? Would they get along as if they'd always known each other, or act like distant relatives? Maybe they wouldn't be friendly toward each other at all. This thought was so disconcerting I divorced myself from the entire train of thought and joined the conversation, reveling in spending time with the boys. Mother-guilt cast a shadow on my heart when I considered my preoccupation since Mitch's death; it was time I rejoined my remaining family.

I didn't open the notebook again for a week.

Grandma Effie says the light of day is harsh on secrets and I can feel safe telling her anything, but I just change the subject and keep my lips zipped. Dad told her what he told everyone else in town: Aunt Audrey had a hysterectomy and she needs someone to live with her in Madison until she's fully recovered. Since Marcia had to enroll in school down there to stay for Audrey's recovery period of four to six weeks, Dad decided to let her finish out the spring semester there so she wouldn't have to make up whatever work she'd miss up here. He says it's important to believe this so we don't say the wrong thing.

He is also afraid Grandma Effie would forget about being secretive and tell one of her old biddy friends at the bingo hall, so even though he wasn't in the habit of keeping such large secrets from his mother, he didn't see any other alternative.

"There's my boy," she says as I trundle through her door after school, "Are you hungry?"

Her house is between the school and our house, so Marcia and I had a habit of visiting on our way home and I'd shovel the walk if it had snowed that day. Now I stop by every day without Marcia and I have to remember not to hold the door for an extra second because there is no one else waiting to walk through it.

"Hi, Grandma. I'm starving." This is always my answer because it earns a huge grin from Grandma.

"Well, you're a growing boy. Let's have a snack and a chat." She has usually already set out placemats and plates. "How was school today?"

I watched her bustle around the kitchen, pouring milk and cutting sandwiches into tiny triangles. "It was okay. You would have liked our Home Ec class today—Mrs. Pendergast told us how to make pot roast."

"Pot roast! My word, that's a complicated dish for a kid to make. Are you making it in class? Do you have time to make an entire pot roast?"

"They changed the class schedule around so we'll have Home Ec first thing in the morning tomorrow, then we'll have it again at the end of the day. We get to bring our pot roasts home, so you're invited to dinner at our house tomorrow night and I'll be doing the cooking." Grandma is old school, of course, so she doesn't think men can cook. I enjoy surprising her.

"Well, that will be swell. Why don't I pick you up after school tomorrow, and drive you home? I'll help you set the table and we'll have dinner all ready when your mom and dad get home."

"Thanks, Grandma, that will be just groovy," I grinned. She always laughs when I say groovy or neat.

"Have you heard from your sister?"

"We talk every night. You can call her any time at Aunt Audrey's. She likes it there so much she said she might get a job after school and stay for the summer."

"My word! I can't reckon a fifteen year old girl staying so far from home. How is your Aunt Audrey's recovery?"

"She sounds fine. She's glad to have Marcia there to help her. She says they're like college roommates." I was on unsafe ground, trying to make sure I didn't slip up and mention Audrey's job, since she was supposed to be off for her 'recovery', and I had to remember Audrey was the one supposedly taking it easy and Marcia was the caregiver. I changed the subject. "How did you do at bingo last night?"

"Well, I almost hit on five cards but then Gertrude and Millie both yelled out 'bingo'. They bingo-ed on a B14 and I was waiting for a B13. So aggravating!"

"I wish I could go to bingo with you sometime. It sounds like fun."

"You can when you're eighteen, but I expect you won't feel like hanging around with your old grandma by then. You're a good boy to visit me even now, instead of chumming around with your pals."

"I don't have many pals, Gram. I keep to myself except for football." This was true; Marcia and I were a society unto ourselves and we hung out with one or two other people until they bored us, and we'd be between friends for a while. I had a feeling we'd be between friends for a long stretch this time.

"Well, you have your sister. You two are better friends than any siblings I've ever known, including your father and your uncle David."

I finished up my sandwiches and cleared the table. Marcia usually washed our dishes but since she wasn't here I took over that duty so Grandma wouldn't have to do it after I left. "Thanks for the snack, Grandma. I've gotta go do some homework before dinner."

"You're welcome, Mitch. I'll see you tomorrow after school. I'll pick you up in the Buick." She hugged me quick through my winter coat and I flashed on what it might feel like if she knew what had happened on Homecoming Night. Losing her steady approval and letting her down would be worse than going to prison for murder.

***

Dad has been sleeping on the couch. I didn't think it was such a big deal but Marcia flipped her lid when I told her.

"Think about it for a minute," she said. "Dad would not sleep on the couch because it's not economical."

"He said he has a sore back."

"I disagree," she sounded stubborn. "Do you really think he would carry his pillow and a blanket out to the couch, only to fold the blanket up again in the morning and

101

put the pillow back on his bed?" She was right. Dad hated to see wasted effort of any kind so he must have had a good reason for sleeping by himself.

"They're probably upset about The Situation," Marcia continued. Whenever she said 'the situation' I could hear her capitalizing it. "You should make sure they spend time with each other."

"They live together!"

"I know, I mean spend fun time together, like dinner dates and movies and stuff. I don't want to be the reason they split up! This year is already crazy enough and I don't want anyone else to have to live with the consequences of The Situation."

I got her calmed down by promising her I'd finagle ways to get them out on dates. As Gram would say, now I'm in a pickle.

Reading the notebook leaves me spent, experiencing the anxiety and doubt all over again along with Mitch.   I'm sequestered in the laundry room, enjoying the rare gift of a day to myself when the store isn't open.   The urge to read Mitch's words supersedes my virtuous housecleaning intentions as I sink to the floor and curl up with the book, the laundry spinning and thumping, creating a soothing cocoon of sound.

March 1976

What comes first: friends or family? Apparently family, although I could argue Marcia is also my best friend. We have our moments like all brothers and sisters but we get along 95% of the time. Sometimes no one else knows we're arguing because we just do it with our eyes or by turning our backs on each other. Usually we use words, though, because that's less intense. It's painful when Marcia turns her back on me or shoots daggers from her eyes. I think my heart stops for a few seconds when she does that.

When Marcia comes home will she think I look crazy? She says I'll think she's fat but I would never think that even if she was. I told her we can do sit-ups together every morning until she feels like her old self.

"I can't imagine being able to do sit-ups right now," she said. "This is like having a soccer ball between my hip bones, right in the way for tucking my knees up close. And it'll just get worse! Imagine having a watermelon in your lap while you're trying to do sit-ups."

104

"It won't be forever; you'll come home, we'll do our sit-ups and everything will be fine."

"I hope so, M."

"It's true, M, don't worry. You can count on me."

"I do, every day."

***

Mom and Dad went out on a date. I bought them tickets to the movies, good for any show this whole month, and it worked. They went to dinner and the movies and they slept in the same bed that night. And the next night. No more nights have passed yet but I'm sure Dad will keep sleeping in bed because Marcia's right, it's highly inefficient to carry the bedding back and forth to the couch every night and morning.

I'm glad Mom and Dad are working things out. M and I have so much to deal with already, we just don't have the resources to handle another crisis. I got that phrase from Dad and I'm going to practice using it now so I can say it when I'm a detective.

***

I think about two things and two things only: Marcia, then Howard. Then Marcia, then Howard. It makes me dizzy. My thoughts are like little hamsters running on the same wheel, climbing through the same tubes, traveling the same path every day. Hell, every few minutes.

Marcia's life has been changed forever. I worry she

won't get over this, won't get past the memory of being pregnant and giving birth, then leaving the baby with people she doesn't even know. Mom says it'll seem like a speed bump, but I don't see how such a big experience can shrink down that small. And, I've been reading about rape and rape victims in the library. I pretended I was doing some research for an essay. Anyway, some rape victims never recover from the horror. Marcia may never be able to trust someone enough to marry him and have a family. One book said rape is worse than murder because it's an attack on the most basic, personal level and the victim has to live with the memory. At least the murder victim doesn't have to figure out how to continue living a normal life after being murdered. And one book said most victims know their attackers, and the majority of attackers are over forty years old.

Howard must have been an over achiever.

And what did Howard think? That he could attack my sister, hurt her, stick his thing inside her and I would just stand by and let it happen? Did he think we would still be *friends*? It pisses me off, thinking about what might have happened if I didn't walk into the room that night and see Marcia's face. Howard would have lived and he'd keep playing football, going to school, visiting our house, and we'd both have to look at him every day knowing what he'd done.

I can't believe Howard Barstow did this to my sister. I'm beyond pissed off—I don't even know what to call this level of anger. I'm not usually an angry guy, even playing football I'd apologize if I rammed into someone and I'd always give them a hand up and brush them off. If I could get on the field now and pretend the other team was a line-up of Howard Barstows I'd probably cream them all and win the game by myself.

Sometimes when I'm in Marquette I see Howard walking down the street. Last week I thought I saw him about a football field length ahead of me on Washington Street, his blocky head covered with a red toque and his puffy blue winter coat making his legs look like saplings. Then he turned around and it wasn't Howard at all and I realized his coat wasn't even blue. It was black.

This is how my subconscious keeps pulling my thoughts back to Howard.

Thinking I'm seeing Howard makes me feel like I'm going crazy and I'll end up being one of those people who wanders around arguing with invisible enemies or laughing at jokes no one else can hear. Then I get mad because Howard has effectively ruined Marcia's life and if I go crazy then he's ruined my life too, and it's all his fault. I blame Howard for creating the situation that made me angry enough to strangle the future right out of him.

The next well-worn groove in this thought pattern rut is a putrid stew of guilt, regret, sadness and rage. My head spins and my guts churn to the rhythm of the images flashing through my mind. All sorts of images play on an unending reel: images of Howard and me in school, in the tree house, playing football, all the big times and small times we had over the years, and his face at the end, surprised, shocked, panicked, desperate, fighting, and finally blank, relaxed, sinking out of sight.

Once I recover, my mind turns to Marcia, to the events of that night, and the question I've asked myself at least a thousand times since then: would I do the same thing if I had it to do over? It's hard to admit, but yes I would. I am not the kind of guy who can stand by and allow someone to treat my sister like a piece of meat and I wish I had the courage to turn myself in and justify my actions to a judge and jury but I am not that strong.

But wait a minute. I have never truly considered what would have happened if I had only given Howdy a black eye and a cursing, maybe some bruised ribs or a broken arm. I enjoy picturing this, imagining watching him apologize and beg for mercy, and letting him go on apologizing forever. Maybe it would have been crueler to let him live. But if I'd let him live, not only would he have had to live with his actions, Marcia would have to see him around town, in school, at sporting events. I tried to imagine the terror Marcia would have felt every time she and Howdy crossed paths after the attack.

This is how I know I did the right thing. I removed the possibility of a second attack, I removed the possibility of Howdy attacking other girls, and I removed the possibility of Marcia encountering Howard and being forced to remember and relive that night.

As usual after following the tangled threads of my thoughts I am exhausted. So I turn out the light and feel the inexorable pull of the same dreaded familiar thoughts again, and again, and yet again. And then the sun rises and I get dressed and I begin another day of private mental torture.

Three days passed before I realized my mind was firmly ensconced in 1975 and I had no clear recollection of my activities or any conversations I'd had since I'd last read Mitch's words. I must have opened the store, I mused, since today was Thursday and I'd last read the notebook on Monday. I stood in the store now, and it appeared freshly dusted, hot coffee ready to pour when Mabel came in.

A shadow fell across the doorway and it took me a moment to recognize Curtis Langley, Mitch's boss.

"Hiya Marcia, how you holding up, kid?" I hadn't seen Curtis since the funeral, where I was told he cried like a baby, but his presence there registered with me only after reading the guest book a week after the event. His glance took in the entire store, verifying we were the only two inside.

Hi, Curtis. I'm muddling through. Every day is a teeny tiny bit easier than the day before." I know people only want to hear good news, uplifting and inspiring news, but this is the best I can offer without blatantly lying.

"Yeah, we're muddling through, too. At the station. It's not the same, I know, but...," His long face grows longer.

"It's okay, Curtis, I know you guys were close. Probably as close as family, just in a different way."

Curtis rested his hands, holding a file folder, on the counter and studied the blank manila for a moment, shoulders curved into the signature posture of tall people.

"Oh, yeah!" He seemed startled. "I almost forgot why I came in. This file was discovered after the accident," his eyes apologized as he said the word in the most delicate way a large man can, "and it's not a Department file. It's not even one of our file folders. I figure Mitch was doing some personal investigating, maybe for a private individual. Anyhow, you're his next of kin and this is personal property." He slid the file across the counter to me.

"Thank you, Curtis," I said, looking away as I saw his eyes fill. Cops aren't supposed to cry, I thought, even as my own throat closed and I fought back the urge to sob. I breathed forcefully through my nose.

"I'm so sorry, Marcia," Curtis said, sandpaper in his voice. "I'm sorry for your loss. And I should have brought this file by earlier, but I didn't want to intrude, and then it got misplaced for a while, and I just found it the other day..."

I covered his hand with mine. "It's okay, Curtis. I appreciate your bringing it here now. And I'm sorry for your loss, as well. We've both lost a great friend and brother," I patted his arm and he turned to leave the store, ducking beneath the bell as he opened the door.

I blew my nose and opened the file. Mitch's blocky printing, nearly unchanged in the past thirty-five years, confronted me with two lists: a list of facts and a list of questions. The second page contained notes.

Facts:
1. DOB: 07/17/1976
2. Adoption Agency: Children's Aid Society, Madison
3. Original birth certificate listed Marcia as mother and Harold Bartholemew as father.

Questions:
1. Is Children's Aid Society still in operation?

—Yes. Still at same address—they purchased the adjacent building and expanded their footprint in 1992. Now have planned parenthood facilities and some welfare programs.

2. Who is in charge of records/archives?

Records from 1976 are archived. Mrs. Melody Wiseman runs the file room. All requests must meet her approval before records can be accessed.

3. Appointment: 3 p.m., Wednesday, March 18, 2009

Notes:

—will need proof of my relationship to Marcia

—Melody Wiseman has no criminal record; neither does her husband Robert.

—she has no children—maybe she put one up for adoption? Might work in our favor.

The first thing I noticed was the date of the appointment: three days after Mitch's accident. I scanned the page again, this time at a slower pace, and realized he'd been searching for Daisy.

"Only Mitch," I whispered, finishing the sentence in my head. Only Mitch would have known that finding Daisy would help me heal and move beyond Howard's death.

I closed the file and regarded it, pacing back and

forth while it rested on the counter.   It held the beginnings of hope, the possibility of locating the infant (thirty-five-year-old woman, I corrected myself) I'd abandoned. Would she want me to find her? Maybe she was perfectly happy, content with her adoptive family. Maybe she had a family of her own already. I wondered if she did, and if she'd ever considered putting her own child up for adoption. Was she pro-life? Did she realize she was adopted?   If she didn't realize it, then the entire adoption had no impact on her life whatsoever.

If she did realize it, did she feel as if something was missing from her own life, like I did? I hoped she'd never had any medical issues, resolvable only by obtaining her parents' medical histories. Was she happy?

That's all I really need to know, I thought.

The file maintained its innocence, offering no advice on whether to continue Mitch's investigation or not, and I shoved it into my tote bag next to his notebook.

April 1976

I miss Marcia. I miss her so bad, like I've lost an arm or my shadow. It's like I've lost mass and am no longer substantial enough to withstand regular daily life. Whenever I think of her, which is all the time, I see her face that night. She looked horrified, shocked, scared, and in pain all at the same time. My stomach twists just thinking about it. Then when I saw the blood on the bed and noticed her clothes were all jumbled up, I knew I had to find Howdy. Marcia had tears running down her face but she was barely breathing. She'll be back in another three months—actually, 94 days, and it just seems so long.

We talk on the phone almost every day, in the evenings after supper, and she sounds brave and happy but I know she isn't. We're only allowed to talk for three minutes because it's long distance. I use Mom's kitchen timer, setting it for one hair short of three minutes to make sure we don't stray into the fourth minute and get charged for it, too.

Sometimes we just sit on the phone and let the silence do the talking for us because we never really need to use words. We just use them to be polite when others are around because they would never understand our twin talk. I'm sure no one would believe we were really communicating without words but I can tell by the rhythm and volume of Marcia's breathing how her day was, if she's happy or sad, hungry, excited or tired. Right now she's tired, sad and feeling defeated and deflated, even though she says she looks like she has a beach ball under her shirt. She is making the best of staying at Aunt Audrey's, which isn't bad overall, and she's going to school there so when she comes back this summer she'll be all caught up and able to start school with me again in the fall.

Mom always takes the phone when I'm finished and tells Marcia to stay on task, as if Marcia isn't a natural straight-A student already and is genetically incapable of earning a B.

Dad sometimes takes the phone after Mom, if he happens to be passing through the kitchen at the right moment, and he always says "hang in there, baby" with a big sigh. Dad has the hardest time with the situation, not counting myself, but he doesn't have all the facts. I think he has logically concluded what happened, but isn't sure how it happened or who made it happen. Plus, he doesn't want to face anything so horrendous. Mr. Mattson would say this type of reasoning wouldn't hold up in court. It's called circumstantial evidence and that's not enough for a murder conviction. Anyway, who's to say Howdy didn't just up and walk away? People do that sometimes.

Dad once asked me if we might run into Howard Barstow someday around town and I said "I wouldn't waste my time worrying about that." He nodded and looked somehow more relieved and more worried at the same time. Dad is a believer in economy in all of its forms. He's always seeking the shortest route, the most efficient schedule or the best way to ration staples. He says the best economic efficiency he's encountered so far was having twins, thereby accomplishing his wish for a healthy family of four in half the allotted time.

I think my efficient removal of Howard Barstow impressed him but it's something he'll never be able to acknowledge.

Hastings Junction is a small town and most people know most other people's business, almost right down to which pair of underwear they're wearing at a given moment. I'm sure I could recognize anyone in this town from a split-second shot, either in profile or from behind, and I could recognize most people from a silhouette. Especially if they moved—people move in distinct ways, waving their arms, shrugging their shoulders, shaking their heads. I've always noticed small inconsistencies, too, such as a mis-buttoned coat or a smudge of dirt on the knee of someone's trousers.

Our Home Ec teacher, Mrs. Pendergast, says my attention to detail will help me go far in this world. She's a nice old lady but she's not too bright. The first day Marcia and I were in her class she asked us, with a straight face, "Are you identical twins?"

We looked at each other as if meeting for the first time, looking into each other's faces as if into mirrors, craning our heads around to study each other from all angles, and then we replied in unison, "We're seven eighths identical and one eighth fraternal."

Mrs. Pendergast clasped her hands and said, "My land, I've never heard of that. That is *so interesting.*"

We shrugged and said together, "It's just biology."

Mom said it wasn't nice to torture poor Mrs. Pendergast that way, but I told Mom that at least we don't call her Mrs. Penis Grasp, which is what the other kids call her behind her back. Mom just shook her head and said, "Well, I should hope not."

Since Howdy's been gone I've been hanging loose, not really palling around with anyone. He disappeared on Homecoming Night, which marked the end of football season and the beginning of winter. Howdy's parents call me sometimes to ask if I've heard from him. My reply is always the same: "Not yet, but when I do, I'll let you know straight away." I am always extremely careful to say *when* instead of *if* because if Howdy's parents are the type of people who notice tiny details they'll be sure to pick up on that one. Besides, *if* I were to hear from Howdy I'd have to face the reality of a psychotic break. His parents would be the least of my worries.

I feel bad about his parents, I really do, because

Howard was a good boy and everyone figured he'd go to college and become a lawyer. He could win any argument hands down, and he could even argue for the side he didn't agree with and still win. Howdy was into the girls pretty heavy, though. He'd bragged to me the week before Homecoming that he'd already scored three times with girls from other towns after our football games. Marcia doesn't know about those girls and I'm not going to tell her.

I knew about Howard's reputation back then, of course I knew. In a town the size of Hastings Junction, in 1975, pre-Cable TV, pre-internet, pre-private phone lines, we all kept close track of every citizen's comings and goings. The older generation always said they had to follow the gossip just to keep their minds sharp, but the younger generation didn't disguise or excuse their base curiosity. We just talked about people.

Howard "kept a girl" as I'd heard he liked to say, in every opposing football team's town so he'd have something to do during away games. His reputation far outreached our small territory, stretching beyond Iron Mountain to Ontonagon in the west, and east as far as Sault Ste. Marie.

But I'd believed I had his heart.

Howard's parents have no idea Marcia isn't visiting Aunt Audrey to assist her while recovering from surgery. The whole town believes that cockamamie story, which is pretty incredible when you consider how much everyone knows about everyone here. For instance, Mrs. Walton is the mayor's wife and is always acting like she's perfect and has never done anything wrong, but everyone knows she's a product of an affair her mother had with the guy across the street. It's not her fault, but she doesn't need to be so high and mighty all the time. And the man who owns the grocery store, Mr. Brand, always appears well dressed, not a hair out of place (although I did notice a frayed cuff on his dress shirt once) but he's actually a falling-down drunk most week nights after the store closes. If you go to his house and knock on the door and he doesn't answer, odds are he's pissed up and avoiding company. There have been half brothers and sisters over the years who didn't realize they were related to each other until they'd started dating and their parents sat them down and explained history, and there've been more than a few babies born six or seven months after a wedding involving someone other than the biological father.

I used to be a pretty talkative kid, rambling on about everything that crossed my mind all day long kind of like I'm doing here, but now I run through everything I'm about to say before I say it to make sure I don't spill any beans. If even one little bean gets spilled the whole bag will come tumbling out. That's why I want to keep writing it all down, so I can get it out of my system without anyone finding out. After I finish the whole story I might burn it or store it in the attic where it will eventually turn yellow and fade to nothing.

***

My full name is Mitchell Darwin Harrison III. Gramps used to call me 3 when he was alive. He called Dad 2, claiming it was easier than having a Mitchell, a Mitch and a Mitchie running around. Dad said Grandpa didn't want to be referred to as Old Mitch, but I didn't mind being called 3. I thought it sounded groovy. Mom said it sounded like I came off an assembly line.

Gramps is kind of the reason Howard Barstow is resting in peace in the swamp behind his dad's hunting camp. The minute I saw Marcia's face that night and realized what had happened, I heard Grandpa's standard phrase: "Take care of your sister, 3. That's your job." I heard his voice so clearly I wouldn't have been surprised if I'd looked sideways and he'd been standing at my elbow. "You have to take care of this. You're supposed to watch out for your sister," he would have said.

Later, with Howard resting uncomfortably beneath a partially uprooted tangle of tag alders, camouflaged under a pile of leaves and already sinking slowly into the muck, I felt a warmth spreading through my chest and back as if Gramps was signaling his approval and somehow patting me on the back or shaking my hand with his patent, "Atta boy, 3. You set things right."

Grandpa believed men were put on this earth to make sure women are protected and safe. He always opened the car door for Grandma even after his driver's license was revoked and she had to drive him to his doctor appointments. "There's no indignity in letting my wife drive me around," said Gramps, "but there's also no reason she has to pump the gas or open her own door." He always complimented Grandma on her fine cooking and her tidy house. "I'm lucky she lets me live here," he'd say, "especially after I tromped in with muddy boots this morning."

Gram would grin and wave his comments aside, shaking her head at his antics. "One of these days I'll teach you how to mop the floor," she'd threaten, "so you can clean up after yourself."

"I'm much too old to mop floors!" He'd protest, "That's why I married such a young dish, to take care of me." He'd wink and say, "Let's hope we never see the day an old man like me has to mop the floor." And we never did—Gramps died when Marcia and I were twelve and he was eighty-seven, leaving Grandma Effie alone at seventy-eight.

Dad worried about Gram at first, which is why Marcia and I started stopping by her place on our way home from school. "It'll give her something to look forward to," said Dad. "She loves feeding growing boys and girls." He didn't worry for long, though, because Gram started playing bingo and meeting her friends for lunch and card games, and she started saying things like, "Mitch and I had a good, long run. I'm lucky to have had such a long and happy marriage." It's true she seemed sadder than before, not quite as lit up, but mainly she was still the same old Grandma Effie. And I knew as well as Dad that knowing the truth about the situation would not improve Gram's life one bit.

I wondered about Daisy every day now, vacillating between calling Melody Wiseman to start the process of locating my daughter or ignoring the information, opting to believe Daisy lead a safe and happy life and my appearance would be either an unwelcome interruption or a disastrous invasion. This list of two items appeared in my imagination in Mitch's economic printing, an invisible third page in his file entitled Options.

Sometimes I allowed myself to think Daisy was looking for me and suffering the same doubts about my reaction, and several times I nearly picked up the phone to dial the agency.

Did Daisy experience similar curiosity? Not knowing was almost enough to propel me to call Melody, now a familiar name, but invariably I froze before acting.

I think Mom is disappointed about Marcia. She won't come out and say so, and I don't think she's disappointed *in* Marcia exactly, but disappointed *for* her. Mom says Marcia's pregnancy and adoption is just a speed bump in her life and that she'll look back on this year one day in the future and it will seem like it happened to someone else. I hope that's what Marcia thinks some day. It feels to me like the longest night ever—like this is all one big continuation of Homecoming Night, which began as a bright autumn morning smelling like wet leaves and ended with a brief, informal eulogy said by me over my friend as he sank slowly into the swamp, the only witness a skittish rabbit peeking from the edge where the ground rises. The night was cool, not quite crisp, and the almost full moon provided just enough light to bury someone and carve RIP at the base of the closest tree.

Sometimes I worry about myself: am I a true killer? Technically I am, although I don't feel like one; I feel like a fellow who defended his sister when another fellow hurt her. The only way I knew to even the score was to make sure

Howdy would never hurt another girl. One look at Marcia's face that night told me her life had already changed forever; how could I let Howdy continue to walk the planet, unchanged and most likely looking for more girls to force himself on? I even thought about the girls he'd told me about before, the ones he said he'd scored, and wondered if they'd been willing or if he'd just decided for them.

You think you know a person, especially here in this tiny little town, and especially when it's someone who was born and raised here right alongside you, going to day care and then kindergarten and then grade school and high school, sleeping over nights, celebrating birthdays and holidays with each other's families. The farther I go down this mental path, marveling at Howard's true personality, the more sickness I feel in my own gut. It starts as a mild sensation of nausea then slowly morphs into a feeling of imminent vomit as I realize my own personality isn't known to anyone either and it never can be.

Sure, Marcia knows me. This hardly counts because the day she doesn't know me will be the day one of us dies. She knows what I did and she knows I'm not a dangerous bloodthirsty criminal killer perpetrator. She knows, and Dad knows without knowing he knows. I think his notion of what I did that night remains vague as if there's a barrier of insulation between the sad, despicable facts and his acknowledgement of them.

I'm writing in circles now, accomplishing nothing. I'm frustrated with my own ability to set all of this behind me and move on, yet I know it's huge and life changing and I can't very well say to myself, "It's over, time to think about tomorrow," and forget about it. Maybe it'll get easier when Marcia moves back home and things return to normal. As normal as possible without Howdy, that is.

Mabel gazed into my eyes, which was a bit unsettling until I figured out she was assessing my mood before she said her next words.

"Do you believe in pre-ordained life?"

"What do you mean?"

"You know, like fate. Like, do you believe that your life is already mapped out for you, and Mitch's life was mapped out for him, and he was supposed to perish in that accident all along, but no one knew it?"

"Um...no."

"Now, don't discount this notion out of hand, Marsh. There are far too many coincidences in this world to say things aren't pre-ordained. Hell, even the way I met Henry, the old battle axe, pretty much cemented our future together."

Relieved for the slight change in subject, I pursued this tangent. "How did you meet?"

"I'll tell you, but then you might find yourself viewing your life in a whole new light," she shrugged.

"I'll take my chances," I smiled at her, suddenly exhausted. "Speak."

"Well, I was six years old, playing kick the can with my cousins and some neighborhood kids. Henry and his family had moved into the house down the street about two weeks prior to that, but none of us had met him yet. He was this quiet, shy kid who hid behind the curtains in the house, spying on us running around the neighborhood, too scared to come out and play," she waved her hand dismissively. "You know, a real wuss."

"I feel bad for him, too shy to come outside," I said.

"Yeah well, he lost all humility when he grew up and started drinking and beating-" she cleared her throat. "Anyway. So, we decided to play a game of Red Rover for a change, but we were wishing we had more kids. One of my cousins dared me to knock on Henry's door and invite him to join us."

"Oh, that's so cool, you invited him to join you in a game of Red Rover, and he ended up inviting you to join him for eternity," I fluttered my eyelashes at her, clasping my hands near my heart.

"Oh, stop it. Don't be an idiot. No, that's not how it happened. I walked into his house, and saw a picture of myself on his mantel." She sat back, awaiting my reaction.

"What?! How in the world did a photo of you appear on his mantel?"

"That was my question exactly. Henry's mother opened the door, and I took a deep breath and tried to ask her if Henry could come out to play, but I stopped mid-sentence when I saw the photo. What I said ended up sounding something like: Hello, my name is Mabel Montrose and I was wondering—hey, where did you get that photo on your mantel?

"Henry's poor mother was confused for a moment, until she took a closer look at me, and then she said, 'well, my goodness, you're the little girl from the train station' which confused me, so we both stood there staring at the photo until Henry came out and asked what was going on."

"So, how did she get that photo?"

"She had taken the photo one day when she was at the train station to see her husband off, and I was there waiting for my grandmother to arrive. Apparently I was standing near the edge of the platform, staring down the tracks, willing the train to appear. She said my facial expression was the personification of anticipation. I had no idea what she meant, of course, but I memorized it and skipped home to find out if this was a good thing or a bad thing."

"And this is what illustrated to you—pardon the pun—that you and Henry were fated to be together? This chance encounter on the train platform with Henry's mother?"

"Well, yes. Think about it. His mother had been looking at my face for two years. They lived across town when Henry's dad traveled all the time, and when he got a promotion and no longer had to take a weekly train, they were able to afford a nicer house, right in my neighborhood."

"What if you hadn't believed in fate? What if you had not cultivated any type of relationship with Henry, and met someone else...a coworker or something...and married him?"

"If I'd fought it, it still would have happened. The marriage, the baby, the baby's death, the whole lot. It just would have been more heartbreaking because of my resistance. You just have to go with the flow, Marsh. Everything is pre-ordained."

"I can't believe, and won't believe, that Mitch was meant to die at the age of 50. It's wrong, it's unfair, and it makes me feel like our entire lives were lived without purpose."

"It's fate."

I murdered my friend. My name is Mitchell Darwin Harrison III and I'm a B and C student and a damn good football player. I wear the green and gold with pride, jogging out on the field to the school song, keeping a sharp eye on the cheerleaders screaming about the Eagles, watching the Eagle mascot strut around the field. Football is pretty big here; I'm the wide receiver, number 31, and Howard was the quarterback, number 17. Life was good and we were winning. The newspaper called us supersonic.

Except now I've murdered my friend, my quarterback, so now the newspaper is saying things like STAR QUARTERBACK MISSING, PRESUMED DEAD because it's been over six months and what are the odds a teenage boy would still be alive after so much time? Howard's parents are upset the newspaper is printing this, squashing their hope right out in public like that, but just as we're learning in Mr. Mattson's class, there's freedom of the press and they like to use it every day.

I wonder if President Nixon feels as crummy as I do. His problems aren't only printed in a small-town newspaper, they're broadcast across the whole USA. You can't turn on the TV right now without hearing the word Watergate. Mr. Mattson said it's hard to teach a class about how government is supposed to work when the President is publicly humiliating himself and, by extension, his whole country. Mr. Ford is actually our president now, which is confusing because former presidents are still called Mr. President, but President Ford will surely do a better job than President Nixon.

One good thing about living here in the UP, Dad says, is we are insulated from the shenanigans in Washington, DC. He's always explaining how our local economy is in a state of perpetual depression and reacts so slowly to the economic trends, we experience less severe swings because when the 'real' economy swings way up, ours just starts to gently curve upward and then the real economy swings downward so we crest and then begin to descend. Our wages here don't change much. I think people get cost of living raises but they're just a few pennies per hour and not enough to cover the real cost of living unless they continue to live here where the costs rise but not as fast. It's kind of like our economy has arthritis and it moves slower than a young, fit economy. I'm not sure how different this is from living in the rest of the country but I think I'd be stressed out living on an economic roller coaster.

It's relaxing to worry about something like the economy instead of wondering if I'm mentally unstable or completely heartless or otherwise messed up.

My hands are shaking so bad I can hardly write. The cops were just here asking questions of me, Howard's best friend and teammate, about a picture and a piece of paper they found. The Barstows think the picture and note might have fallen out of Howard's wallet. This is how everything went down:

The cops knocked on the door and my dad welcomed them in, (*welcomed them!*) and we all sat in the living room around the coffee table. I tried to act casual but I needed to take really deep, slow breaths. I must have sounded like I had just finished exercising or something.

"We're sorry to bother you folks," started the first officer, Mr. Dean, according to his badge. We didn't know these cops; they were from Marquette because Howard's case was referred to a larger police department and theirs is the closest.

"We found these items in the ditch along Old Mill Road," the second officer, Mr. Tucker, pulled two plastic bags out of his pocket, one containing the photo and the other holding some kind of receipt or note.

"Howard's parents thought maybe this picture and note came from Howard's wallet," said Officer Dean, "and they thought you might be able to identify them, Mitch." The two bags were on the coffee table in front of me.

"Can I touch them?" I asked.

"Oh yes, just keep them in the bags. You can turn

them over or whatever you need to do, as long as we keep them in the bags."

I picked up the photo and studied the school portrait of Becky Smithers. She lives two blocks from Howard and has had a crush on him since he learned to talk and announced to the entire day care center that Becky was his wife and no one else could play with her. She's a year ahead of us in school, but only five months older than Howard.

I felt everyone's eyes on me, studying me even more intently as I gazed at Becky's best smile.

The back of the photo featured Becky's rounded handwriting and a brief message: H—Stay true to yourself and loyal to your friends. To the end, YW, Becky.

I set the photo back on the coffee table and continued to stare into Becky's eyes.

"Well? Is it from Howdy's wallet, Mitch?" Mom seemed nervous, fluttering her hand up near her throat.

"Yeah, I'm pretty sure it is," I said, glancing up at Officer Dean. "Becky and Howard always sign notes to each other with YW or YH, meaning your wife or your husband, because of a joke back when we were all in day care together. I don't know of anyone else she would write to and sign YW. And, she is writing to someone named 'H'. The only other H name we have in the high school is Heather Lukkenen and she and Becky aren't really friends."

"Okay, that's good enough for now. If this thing ever goes to court, could you say you are certain this is from Howard's wallet?" asked Officer Dean.

"I could say with reasonable confidence that yes, this is from Howard's wallet," I replied.

"This boy here watches The Rockford Files," said Dad. Everyone chuckled at this, but my stomach started its usual flipping and twisting.

"What about this note, here?" Prompted Officer Tucker, pushing it closer to me on the table.

I picked it up and studied it. In handwriting similar to Becky's but with enough differences to indicate it wasn't her writing, it said: Howd—Thanx for the moonlit memory! I can't wait for the next time you're in town. You'd better call me, you rascally rabbit! Love ya sweetcheeks, Mandy

"Do you know a Mandy?" asked Officer Tucker.

"Well," I shrugged, "I know Howard had a kind of a girlfriend in Marquette. They got together when we went there for football scrimmages last summer. I forget how many teams showed up, but we played four football games that day against four different teams. Maybe Mandy was from one of the other towns that played—I don't even know if she lived in Marquette or not."

"Well, if she was a girlfriend, didn't he talk about her?"

"She wasn't really a girlfriend, just a kind of girl for him to, you know, mess around with. He just mentioned her one time. I'm surprised he had a note she wrote—it doesn't seem like something he would keep."

The officers both sat back on the couch and looked like they just realized they are in our living room. They swiveled their heads around checking out all of our family photos on the walls, reading the book titles on our shelves, studying the scene out our front windows.

Finally they stood up, like they both heard a silent signal, and thanked Mom and Dad for letting them talk to me.

"Thank you, Mitch, for your valuable information. This might help us solve the whole case," Officer Dean shook my hand before turning to head out the door.

I ran as fast as I could to the bathroom and threw up my lunch, heaving until I thought my socks were going to come out my throat.

The notebook thrums with energy, residing in my tote bag until I can liberate it again. I haven't read a book since I found Mitch's journal, preferring to maintain the illusion of his presence through his words, still somehow fresh on the pages. His presence is different now than it was when he was alive. It's more of a cool space on my right side rather than a warm, solid force.

I've come to regard the notebook as an impetus for change and commencement. It's like peering through a lens and discovering I'm not where I believed I was. My inherent stoicism has most likely crippled my grieving process as I clamped down on my messiest emotions, denying their existence and power. I crave Mitch: his face, his voice, his stolen self. I've lost too much to recover, and the one sickeningly over-used phrase repeating itself in my mind is (inward cringe) Be Here Now. I can't let myself appear new age-y even for a moment, having vocally derided the collective new age hippy dippy culture for years. Preferring action over meditation, I scanned and printed several photos of Mitch, an attempt to manifest his physical self in the only way I can. His images are framed and displayed on our hallway wall, where we can view them from one side of the living room, and one is hanging at the store in a place of honor on the wall behind the cash register. It's the first place people look when they walk through the door, and the photograph shows both of us mugging for the camera, our near-identical expressions and facial features highlighted by the dramatic shadowing in the black and white image.

Having his photos on display, rather than causing grief and turmoil as I'd expected, brings comfort and peace as they offer evidence of my truth. I was once one half of a whole, but I now stand alone.

I try to be as strong as he thought I was.

I've been reduced to hanging out with Ripley and I don't know if things can get much worse unless, of course, someone figures out what happened to Howard. Since Howdy was my main friend and practically my only friend, I've been hibernating all winter long. I had to keep a low profile anyway so I guess it worked out for the best. Yeah, I couldn't have hung out with someone because I would have wanted to talk and that would be a very bad idea.

Ripley started talking to me more last week and today I invited him over after school, including my daily stop at Gram's for a snack. I called ahead so she would be prepared for two hungry boys instead of just one and she was so happy to see us she made my favorite soup: chicken noodle with extra carrots.

I think Gram was thrown for a minute when she saw Ripley, but she recovered quickly because she's so polite. If I ever wonder what to do in a given situation, how to handle something with class, I imagine what Gram would do and I just do that. Anyway, Ripley walked in the door ahead of me with his usual expression of surprise and Gram kind of jumped.

"Oh! Well, you must be Ripley. Come on in," she gestured wide with one arm, pointing vaguely at the kitchen.

"I am Ripley, indeed! And you must be Mitch's Grandmama. It is *so* nice *and* interesting to meet you!" Ripley replied, his eyebrows shooting toward his hairline. The eyebrows combined with his bugging out eyeballs made him appear startled, excited and skeptical all at once. His bugging out eyeballs are the reason we call him Ripley. His real name is Richard Walther, and he used to go by Ricky, but one day Miss Pendergast returned one of his papers with a large A scrawled at the top and his eyes bugged out more than usual and he said, "I can't believe it!" Ever since then, we've called him Ripley instead of Ricky, after Ripley's Believe It Or Not.

"Have a seat here, Ripley, and help yourself to some homemade chicken noodle soup," Gram pulled out a chair for him, handing him a napkin as he sat down. She patted me on the shoulder as she walked behind my chair. "I'm glad you brought your friend over, Mitch."

"Did you see the *news* last night?" Ripley asked. Ripley is a bit annoying with his constant surprise bit. I can't figure out if it's natural or mostly put on, but I don't think he talked like that before we started calling him Ripley. If that's the case I guess we created our own monster so I probably shouldn't complain. And, the entertainment value helps make up for the annoyance factor.

"No, dear, I missed it."

"I was on the phone with Marcia. I missed it, too," I said.

"I couldn't *believe* what they had on the news. My dad said they must have nothing to talk about because they had to resort to reporting about a woman with a pet emu. How could an emu even *be* a pet? Can you *walk* it? No. Can you *ride* it? No. Does it *guard your house*? Well, I guess in some ways it does, because I would be terrified to walk up to a house with a huge bird hanging around outside. I wonder if they have a fence. I think they do. I think they showed it—"

"How is the soup, Ripley?" I flinched at Gram's interruption. I've never witnessed her interrupt anyone before! This proves Ripley is truly annoying.

"Oh, this is almost the *best* soup I've ever *had*. It's almost, but *not quite*, as good as the soup my own grandmama makes. You wouldn't *believe* the soup she makes. Every batch of soup is different and it always has an *unusual* ingredient. *For example*, she made chicken noodle soup one time but it wasn't plain old chicken noodle soup, it was *spicy* chicken noodle soup. It had *chilies* and *peppers* in it, right in there with the chicken and noodles and all the regular old *boring* stuff. Well, all the stuff in this soup right here. Which is *very* tasty, by the way, and—"

"What a grand idea, adding peppers to soup. Your grandmother is quite clever, Ripley," said Gram.

I just sat there through this entire exchange, bopping

my head back and forth like a tennis fan at Wimbledon and thinking about Ripley's puppy dog ways. After a while I stopped hearing their words and let the general tone of conversation flow around and through me without hearing any clear words. Ripley's been following me around since we were little kids, waiting in his back yard for me to emerge from the house, which happened to be across the alley from his. I'd walk out the back door and he'd be standing on the strip of grass in the middle of the alley, inviting me to play ball or ride bikes or climb trees.

Since I was usually heading to Howdy's house, nine times out of ten I'd give Ripley a negative reply. He never let up, though; he continued to accost me without fail every time he saw me walk outside. When Howard disappeared Ripley started a more aggressive tactic, actually knocking on our door and inviting me to various events or dinner at his house. Until this week, I declined. I was mainly afraid of saying too much, but now I feel like I've told this notebook everything so I can move on without worrying so much about incriminating myself.

Besides, hanging with Ripley is slightly less pathetic than hanging by myself. One thing is for sure, I can't hear my own thoughts when he's sitting there jabber jawing.

And Marcia's not here. I guess I'll probably go back to my anti-Ripley ways after she returns.

***

Whoa. It's hard to write, my hand is shaking so badly. The police found Howard.

The headline says 'Barstow Body Recovered' and at first I envisioned him being covered again in mud, or maybe a nice soft comforter, but then I realized with a start he (it—the body) was discovered.

B A R S T O W

BODY RECOVERED

(AP) Police today responded to a report from a birdwatcher and discovered the body of Howard Barstow, 15, son of Ronald and Linda Barstow, reported missing on October 18, 1975. The case has been reopened and resources are being re-dedicated to determine whether or not foul play was committed.

Howard was an honor student at Hastings Junction High School and enjoyed playing football. According to reports from teachers and students, he was always quick with a smile and had something nice to say to everyone. "He showed great promise; I always had high hopes for Howard," said Mr. Gouth, Principal of Hastings Junction High School.

Howard was last seen immediately following the Homecoming football game last October by several of his friends and team members at his family's hunting camp. He left the cabin and never returned.

Howard's parents never wavered in their belief that Howard was still alive. "It's difficult to learn we can no longer hope he walks through the door," said his mother. "But at least we will have closure now."

The funeral will be held at the Superior Funeral Home on May 13 at 7:00 p.m., with visiting hours beginning at 4:00 p.m. The Barstows request donations be made to the ambulance corps and police department in lieu of flowers.

The article contains lots of words but no information. The swamp isn't mentioned; did they find Howard there, or was his body somehow moved to a different location? Maybe an animal had dragged him someplace. Were there strangulation marks on his neck?

I need to know what they know.

***

It's almost time for graduation. This year's senior class, the largest in seven years, has twenty-three graduates. They will honor Howard with a song, a poetry reading and a brief slide show.

I think I want to be a detective.

***

Howard's funeral was what Mom called a typical Yooper small-town kid's funeral. The church was so full, people were crammed into every pew, standing along the main aisle, standing along the side aisles, jammed into the foyer and standing out on the front porch. They propped the door open and hooked up a speaker outside so everyone could hear. All of the businesses shut down during the funeral so everyone could attend.

Afterward, everyone went to the bar and shared stories about Howard. I only had one beer, just to be sociable, but a couple of the fellas had three or four beers.

148

Jeff is the only bartender I know who lets highschoolers drink, but this only applies to us locals. "If you're a football player or a cheerleader, you're old enough in my book," he says. "You can't order anything to go, though, until you're twenty-one." Dad ordered a scotch on the rocks once, but he said it doesn't taste as good in a Styrofoam cup.

Anyway, I was afraid to drink more than one beer because my guts were roiling as usual and I felt kind of stunned. A couple of times I went deaf—my ears were ringing, cancelling out all the singing and laughter and tears. Every teacher and most of Howard's relatives came up to me to shake my hand, to say they can't remember Howard without picturing me next to him and to tell me Howard would be proud of me and to remember him always as I go to college and live my life. I almost lost my lunch a few times. Except I haven't eaten anything all day.

Like I told Marcia on the phone, Howard would have been surprised at the number of people who came to his funeral. I guess he'd expect 'everyone' to be there, but he'd be shocked to see Marissa, a girl from Gwinn he'd shagged a couple of times, and Louise, the clerk at the grocery store who lives in Copper Falls, the next town over. Wacky Walter, the homeless guy from Marquette, showed up at the funeral and the bar. He said Howard always took time to say hello to him when he passed him on the street even though everyone else just walked by like they didn't see him. He rode his three-wheel bicycle all the way here just for the funeral, about 25 miles each way. Howard would be humbled, his mom said, to see Walter make such a huge effort.

Marcia made me describe the whole thing to her so she could picture it. "I should have been there," she said, "but there's no way I could hide my condition now. I feel like a freight train walking down the street. Once I get moving, it's pretty hard to slow down and stop. Yesterday I had so much momentum I missed the door to the library and had to turn around and try again."

Howard's folks had a lot of photos of Howard growing up, all pinned to large boards and displayed at the funeral and then at the bar. I counted a total of 117 photos. My face was in 59 of them, growing up right along with Howard. Sixteen of the photos had all three of us, Marcia usually stuffed between me and Howdy.

I miss him.

***

If I become a detective I want to be an undercover one so I don't have to wear the uniform. It looks stiff and itchy and everyone knows you're a detective or cop when you're wearing a uniform. If I'm supposed to solve murders and stuff, I will have a better chance of getting people to talk if they don't know why I'm talking to them. I'll be able to pick up on all of the little clues they don't know they're giving me while we're spilling their beans.

I'll be the one they call in to interview really difficult criminals. I'll solve crimes we're not even working on by linking the stories of different perpetrators and finding patterns in their methods. I'll be better than Jim Rockford.

I'll be the best detective on the force. I won't let a crime go unsolved.

This will be Howard's secret legacy.

***

The school year is finally ending and my life is almost back to normal. I've stopped waiting for Howard to show up again, grinning that stupid blockhead grin of his. I think this is the end of the grief process or something. We had to learn all about the seven stages of grief in school but I can't remember when it ends. Maybe it never ends.

***

The police interviewed me again. They interviewed everyone who was at Howard's camp on October 18, and some people who weren't at the camp. Bobby McKay told me all about his interview, even the questions the police asked, because he was so freaked out about Howard.

"The cops told me not to discuss it," he panted, "but it's not like you know any more than I do. You just feel so bad when they're asking all these questions, cuz there aren't really any answers. I mean, who wasn't wasted that night? Who could possibly know what time Howard left the cabin and didn't return? For Chrissakes, people were streaming in and out of the cabin all night long!"

I remained silent and let Bobby ramble, telling myself I

151

was helping him let off some steam while I listened for clues. I also noticed what questions the cops were asking—what kind of information they were looking for.

"So you didn't know any of the answers to their questions?" I asked.

"Well, I mean, I knew some names of people who were there that night. I knew what time I got there and I knew I was still there the next morning. I slept on the couch; when I woke up, Margaret Crowley's foot was next to my face! She was sleeping on the floor and had one foot up on the couch. It was freezin' ass cold, though, so her foot didn't stink." He chuckled, shaking his head at the memory. "I thought to myself, 'Bizarre! Margaret's foot is in my face!' but that turned out to be the most normal moment of the day. It also turned out to be my worst hangover ever."

When it came time for my police interview, I stuck to a collection of ignorant answers similar to Bobby's, most of which allowed me to tell the truth, or at least one interpretation of it. *What time did you last see Howard? I don't know for sure. Was Howard drunk when he left the party? I don't know. Did Howard seem to be in a reckless mood? I have no idea. Did Howard leave with anyone? Not that I noticed. Were you Howard's friend?* This one made me catch my breath. *Yes. Yes, I was.*

****

"Have you ever noticed," Dad said, "that nobody in Hastings Junction has ever been convicted of murder?" I never thought about it before, but I guess I always assumed there hadn't been anyone to convict. "You're right, but not for the reason you're thinking. You're thinking no one has been murdered; I'm saying no one has been caught." He stared at the far wall. "George Leitonen was a friend of your grandpa's, and his ex-girlfriend's new boyfriend suffered a mysterious death one night after leaving her house. Nothing ever came of it, but I'm confident George had more than a little involvement."

George is a legend in Hastings Junction. He'd never married or had children, but he'd lived with several girlfriends, which was rare back in his day. Everyone else got married, but George just moved his girlfriends in or out of his house, depending on his mood. Sometimes the girlfriends moved out on their own to nurse their broken arms and defeated dreams and allow their black eyes to heal. If George wasn't beating up one of his girls, he was getting thrown out of the bar for hitting someone who'd insulted a woman. I remember overhearing Grandpa tell stories about George when I was younger and the grown-ups hadn't noticed me listening. "He was a curious blend, our George. A chivalrous woman-beater. You could only trust him to behave himself when he wasn't on the whiskey."

Did George really kill someone right here in Hastings Junction and never get caught?

I didn't recall this particular bit of history, but it sounds plausible, given the hundreds of other crazy things I'd heard about life 'back in the day'. The incongruence between the prudish characters and the memories of wild crimes, adulterous sex and illegitimate children (seems like there's more than one in every family, going back three or four generations) always struck me. Why did older people always act like the younger generations were doing more nefarious deeds than they themselves had done? I recalled one exchange I'd overhead in the book store one day.

"Oh my goodness, did you hear about young Joey Carpenter?" said old biddy number one. "He got *another* girl pregnant! My land, that boy needs a hobby!"

"And what is that girl going to do with a baby? She can barely take care of herself," said old biddy number two, "and her mother was the same way, finding herself in the family way at about the same age."

When the biddies emerged from the stacks to present their purchases to me, I recognized old Mrs. Haakola and averted my eyes to contain my (cruel) laughter. Her marriage to Mr. Haakola had ended when he discovered she'd strayed across the alley to find comfort and passion with Mr. Gunderson, their union producing a child with unmistakably German features to match. By the time Mr. Haakola put the facts together, the child was ten years old and Mr. Gunderson long gone.

June 1976

I thought getting out of school would help me escape Howard's ghost but now that I'm working at Greasy Ted's Gas and Go everyone who stops by asks me who I think killed Howard. Sometimes I feel like he's standing next to me, just behind my right shoulder, pressing into my back and grinning like the devil while I stammer and stutter and hope to hell I don't sound as guilty as I am.

Who would have thought I'd have an invisible friend at sixteen.

Most days I keep busy changing oil and sweeping the shop, stocking the shelves with oil filters and fan belts and organizing the tools on the work bench. Greasy Ted says I can arrange the shop any way I want because he's never found a system that works so he's always hunting for tools. When he's working on a big job, like when he overhauled Mrs. Ginsberg's engine in her '66 Buick, I was his surgical assistant and handed him whichever tool he demanded, slapping it into his outstretched grease-lined palm before he finished uttering the final syllable.

"You're a machine, man," said Ted, grinning his big white grin. It might just look white because it's in the middle of his grease-swiped face. "You're a goddamn machine."

I laughed. "Yeah, I'm a gas pumping, tool handling, shop organizing, oil changing, coffee making goddamn machine." I try to list everything I do now and then in hopes of getting a raise but Ted either never gets the hint or just doesn't want to pay me more.

"I still don't know how you stay so clean. These hands haven't been clean since 1958 when I first started working in this here garage." He studied his hands, back and front, as if he was trying to see through the layer of grease. "I wonder if I have pale hands under all this. I really can't remember."

"Well, I don't think the sun can penetrate a thick coating of grease, so I'm guessing your hands are pretty white."

"I guess I could dip them in gas and clean them off that way." He reached for his shop rag, always hanging from his back pocket, and grabbed a bowl and a nail brush.

An hour later he strutted around the shop, showing off his hands like a bride who'd just had a manicure, remarking about the amazing natural resiliency of human skin and the even more amazing cleaning powers of gasoline.

Mrs. Pendergast pulled up to the pump, the loud *ding*! announcing her arrival and effectively ending Ted's tirade.

"You better get that one, sonny," he winked. "I don't want to soil my tender hands." He fluttered his hands in the air once more like a Broadway performer.

"Hello, Mitch," greeted Mrs. Pendergast. "I didn't know you were working here. Are you learning the mechanics of being a mechanic?"

"Yeah, I mean, you know, I'm changing oil for people and pumping gas. I also rearranged the whole garage so the tools are in a more logical order."

"I'm so glad to hear it! You must have learned that in my class, when we discussed organizing the kitchen tools. It's a lesson you can apply to all facets of life."

"Yep."

"Say, how is Marcia? Is she back from your aunt's yet?"

"No, she'll be back around the end of July sometime," I toed the dirt next to her car. "When my aunt is fully recovered."

"Well, I look forward to having you and your sister together again in my class for one more year," she handed a clutch of bills through the window. "You keep the change, Mitchie. It's a tip," she winked and popped the car into drive.

"Thanks, Mrs. Pendergast! I really appreciate it," my stomach flopped guiltily as I realized Mrs. Pendergast was tipping me because she thought I was a good person. She believed she was tipping an honest, hardworking, non-murderous student. My head buzzed and my ears rang. I repeated a silent chant in my mind: *No one can know. No one can know. No one can know.*

I wonder if I'm going insane. Doesn't repeating the

same thing over and over indicate a form of insanity?

I swear I felt Howard's cold death breath on my neck as she pulled onto the road.

When I turned to walk back into the garage, Greasy Ted was silhouetted in the doorway, a dark figure with a white grin and pale dangling hands the only things showing up against all that darkness and grease.

Well, it's the bicentennial of our country but I don't think it's very exciting without Marcia here. She's still trying to sound cheerful on the phone but I can tell she's forcing herself to smile and pretend everything is alright.

Hastings Junction looks pretty cool right now because the high school art class held a contest to paint all of the power poles along Main Street. The rules were simple: paint from the ground to six feet up, and the colors have to be red, white and blue only. So now the street looks like it's lined with pillars, each one more creative than the one before. I feel like I'm in a parade every time I drive to work. I know Marcia would enjoy riding next to me and waving like Jackie O, pretending to acknowledge her fans along the parade route.

The patriotic decorations, created to make us all feel like partying and celebrating, just make me want to lie down and cry. Maybe I should join the Marines.

The fireworks on the 4th weren't as bright and sparkly as usual. I think maybe my vision has dimmed.

Ted works me hard, especially after I organized his tools. He expects me to keep the shop clean, answer the phone and pump gas for everyone. The goal, according to Ted, is to greet the customer within one minute after they pull up to the pump and ding the bell. If I'm not on the phone I drop the broom or shop rag and sprint out there, grinning like an idiot and blowing sunshine every which way. Last week I startled Mrs. Pendergast and nearly pissed myself laughing.

"Good afternoon, Mrs. Pendergast!" I leapt to her car window, nearly faltering when I landed too close.

"Aagh! Oh, Mitch," she patted her chest. "You appeared out of nowhere. You're like a gas pumping superhero!"

For some reason the mental image of a superhero charging about to pump gas in a timely and professional manner hit me sideways and I laughed so hard I think I scared her again. "Yes, during the week I'm just a mild-mannered gas pumper, but every now and then you might catch a glimpse of...hmm...Fuel Flyer. Or something."

Mrs. Pendergast grinned. "Mitch, you make me miss teaching. And that's really saying something, in the middle of July." I gave her a coupon for a free car wash even though she didn't buy quite enough gas, to make up for the double fright. And I was feeling neighborly after she made me laugh. It felt so good to laugh!

The guilt invaded right after she pulled away and I thought of Marcia, who finds it impossible to see any humor in anything right now. She says she just can't see beyond her belly to anything funny or interesting. Life is bleak when viewed from behind a nine-month time bomb.

"I'm only *sixteen*, Mitch."

"Uh—me too, Marsh."

"I mean, I'm only sixteen and I'm having a baby. Sometimes it's just such a huge thing I can't believe it," she sighed. "Then, of course my gaze drops to this huge...cumbersome...*thing* and I can't *not* believe it."

"You're almost there. Look on the bright side—you're only sixteen."

"That's your bright side? I have lots of time left to make more mistakes? Just imagine what I'll be doing when I'm seventeen." She despaired.

"No, I mean since you're only sixteen, you'll bounce back from this so fast you won't even believe it all happened. You'll have to convince yourself it's a memory and not just a bad dream."

"Yeah, I don't know. The doctor said the same thing but I have my doubts. You haven't seen this...growth. It's more than huge. It's gargantuan. It looks like a medicine ball under my shirt."

"I promise you, Marsh, on all that is twin with us. I'll help you. Everything will be back to normal in plenty of time to enjoy the last part of summer and then *whammo*! We'll be in school again."

"That's another thing. I'm dreading school. Everyone is going to have so many questions. I don't know if I can handle it."

"You can handle it, and anyway, I'll handle it for you. That's my job as your brother. I'll make sure no one bothers you or makes your life miserable," I paused. "Hell, it's the least I can do, since you're giving birth and all."

"You better come down with Mom and Dad when they pick me up. I want your face to be the first one I see."

"You better believe it, M," I had a lump in my throat, and she probably knew it, but I wasn't about to admit it. "I'll be there and you'll be square."

"Better than being round," she said, and I sensed her thin joy before I heard her chuckle.

"Marsh?"

"Yeah."

"You are brave. You're my hero." I whispered so she'd feel the weight of the words. They were so heavy I could barely push them from my heart through my throat and out into the phone.

Grandma Effie is still sharp and she notices details like I do; I figured she'd say something when Marcia didn't even come home to visit on spring break, or when Marcia missed the Fourth of July, but Grandma either bought the line that Marcia liked living in the city so much she got a job and wanted to stay until August, or she knew something was up and she was afraid to ask. Because at first she kept trying to make me talk but after a couple months went by she stopped mentioning it. "Our girl is turning into a city mouse," she'd say when Marcia's name came up. "She likes the glitter, I reckon."

I would nod, "It must be pretty exciting, compared to Hastings Junction."

***

Marcia had a baby girl. She never saw her or held her and will never know her name.

We call her Daisy.

For some reason this brief announcement conjures an image of the hospital room for me and I'm transported back with dizzying speed: scratchy gown, nurse with a mole on her face, too many invasions of my personal space, the sickening realization that I was discarding a person.

Cindy, the thin young nurse with the sunny smile and the shiny blonde hair to go with it, came in the morning after the baby was born with several forms to complete. I'd never before considered where the information came from for a birth certificate (mothers simply filled in the blanks and they became legal documents!) and I found it momentous to install my name on the line after the title 'Mother'.

"I just need you to fill out the name and address lines for you and the father, and you can fill in a name for the baby if you'd like, so she has a better label than Baby

Girl, but you don't have to. The adoptive parents will name her anyway," explained Cindy, smiling like a cheerleader as she bustled around the room.

"I didn't expect to fill out paperwork about the father," my voice carried a tremor I hoped Cindy didn't notice. "I guess I never really thought about this part of the process."

"Oh, just fill out what you know," said Cindy, straightening my bed covers and refilling my water glass. "I've always wondered how many birth certificates are filled in wrong on purpose. And if the truth ever comes to light, if the baby ever finds out who the real biological father is."

"What do you mean?   People fill in false information?"

"Oh, all the time," she waved her hand as if tossing something out the window. "Most people who don't want anyone to know who the father is write something like 'John Doe' or 'David Jones'. But this one lady? She had a sense of humor, or maybe she was a tad bitter, I don't really know, but she wrote 'a foolish man' on the line. I couldn't believe it!"

Cindy prattled on for a few minutes, making sure I was comfortable and asking what I'd like for dinner, while

I neatly printed the name 'Harold Bartholomew' after the title Father. I'd meant to write Howard's name down, but I considered Cindy's comment about the baby discovering who the biological father is and I couldn't take the chance of this baby finding Howard's family before she found me (would she ever look?).

August 1976

Marcia is home. She's **home**. My shadow, my arm, my sister. Now I know Marcia is what gives me substance. Without her, I'd be invisible.

Life is back to normal and I can breathe again. I didn't realize it, but I've been short of breath for the past seven months.

I don't have to think about Howard anymore. Seeing Marcia's face has erased all doubts about Homecoming night. She survived! And she's stronger than before.

I'm putting this notebook away for the last time. I don't need it anymore.

Mitch's account ended just as I remembered the day I'd returned home: our reunion, our reality restored, our bond strengthened.   My stomach gradually unknotted, then knotted again as I numbly considered the notebook and its contents, and my responsibility to Mitch, to Howard, to myself. To Daisy. *And what about Howard's parents?* I thought. *Would reading this book afford them any kind of healing? Some form of closure, perhaps?*

The damage to Mitch's reputation, and by association, mine and Evan's and the boys', not to mention those of our parents and close friends, would be devastating and irreparable. Mitch's hard, honest work for the police force would be overshadowed and maybe even forgotten, or dismissed as a classic example of compensating for past actions (sins, for the religious-minded persecutors in the bunch). How would the many victims' families who Mitch helped through the years feel to learn he had committed murder? Would they see the surrounding circumstances as sufficient support for his heinous act? Would they feel somehow less avenged? Would this information cheapen what small satisfaction they must feel about their settlements?

The notebook rested on the counter. I regarded the innocent cover while I tried to decide its fate. Try as I might, I couldn't think of one positive outcome sharing this book would bring to anyone. Even the small comfort I imagined Howard's parents might feel if they at least gained definitive closure would come at a price, as they realized Howard's childhood friend was also his murderer. *By now, thirty-five years after the fact, the Barstows must have made their own peace with Howard's death*, I thought.

After debating with myself for endless minutes, I realized I don't want to be the custodian of Mitch's crime. His monstrous act, performed in the heat of anger and in my defense, should die with him. *He's already paid back as much as any man possibly could*, I thought, and in a sudden rush of resolution before I could change my mind, I gathered the notebook to my chest in a school-girl hug and went to the back yard, coming to a stop near the fire pit.

"I know you kept this notebook to remind yourself

of the one unspeakable act you committed, M," the sound of my own voice, jarring on such a serene afternoon, projected an air of composure I didn't feel. "You were the best human being I've ever known, and I am honored to have been your twin. I've always tried to live up to your standard, Mitch, and I've fallen short many times. But you already know that," I smiled at this, recalling the secret codes of our communication, unspoken and more intense than any verbal language could be. "I can't and won't be the custodian of this evidence to the contrary; I choose to remember your true self, and I will dedicate myself to helping others remember, too. As long as I am alive, you live on in me."

I lit the crumpled pages I'd torn out to use as kindling, and stood vigil while Mitch's words curled into ashes and floated upward, spiraling away on lazy air currents until I could no longer see them.

The smoke disappeared in the thick fog, and the drizzle that had begun that morning kept the fire at a low, respectable burn.

A movement suddenly caught my eye and I turned to see a woman crossing the yard toward me, purposeful long-legged strides projecting a confidence her face didn't show.

Daphne

I was seven years old jumping rope with Tracy MacArthur on the playground during recess when three other girls joined in. Tracy and I were close; our mothers visited each other several times per week and we played Barbies and invented complicated scenarios that Barbie always solved with flair. The four of us chanted together, taking turns rotating the rope and jumping.

"I just learned a new chant from my cousin. Want to hear it?" asked Jodi. Her pigtails stuck straight out from her head like handlebars.

"Sure," we answered as a group.

"Okay," she cleared her throat. "Just turn the rope at regular speed. I'll say the chant, then someone else jumps in and tells the news." The rest of us looked at each other and I could tell we were all thinking the same thing: we didn't watch the news! "It's not the real news.

You just tell gossip you heard or you make something up. Gossip is always better.   Then after someone jumps in and tells the news, we all guess if it's true or made up."

"We'll try it out," said Lisa, "and if we don't like it we'll go back to Hot Peppers."   Lisa loved bossing everyone around, even the teacher.

Lisa and I started turning the rope, keeping the pace moderate and steady.   Jodi waited through three turns, getting into the rhythm before she darted in and started jumping and chanting.

"Blondie and Dagwood went to town!   Blondie bought an evening gown!"   She sang out clearly. "Dagwood bought some brand new shoes, and then he went home and read the news!"   She looked around, bouncing in time with the rope.   "Get ready! Someone has to jump in with the news!"   She let the rope go around two more times, then repeated her last line, "then he went home and read the news. And the news said..."

Wendy jumped in smoothly as Jodi exited, her long legs like a cricket's, knees pointing every which way. She finished the sentence with a disjointed, but rhyming, report. "The old gas station turned to ash; Papa Bear ran out of cash. Madison High was painted blue and now it looks like it's brand new."

We all guessed correctly the only factual part of Wendy's news report was the first item about the gas station burning down, but it wasn't technically news because it had happened before any of us had started kindergarten and we were already in second grade.

Jodi, who'd apparently appointed herself our leader despite Wendy's glares, clapped her hands to rally us. "Okay people, let's try it again! It gets harder to make up new stuff. I'll start it out again. This time, Wendy can turn the rope so someone else can pop in and tell the news."

"Ooh! I have news I just remembered," Tracy looked at me, but I couldn't read her expression. "Does it have to rhyme?"

"No," said Jodi. "It's more fun if it rhymes, but the real news never rhymes so my cousin said it's okay if that part doesn't rhyme." She jumped, repeating the vignette about Blondie and Dagwood's hot date.

The rest of us listened intently, ready to hear Tracy's news. I was shocked to hear my own name when she started jumping.

"Daphne's not like me and you, but I know this much is true: she's a real nice girl and my best friend, even though she was adopterated." She jumped out, the rope lightly slapping her on the shoulder because I'd stopped turning it.

"Sorry, I couldn't think of a rhyme for adopterated. But it's real news, even though it happened so long ago when she was a baby, because I just heard it yesterday."

"What's adopterated?" Wendy asked.

"You know, like her parents didn't want her so they gave her away and someone else came along and took her home." Tracy said this like it happened all the time, babies lying about abandoned, awaiting rescue. I'd never heard of such a thing, so I challenged her.

"People don't leave babies lying around for someone to take," I said. "And my mom didn't steal me! She's my *mom*."

"People leave their babies all the time!" said Tracy. "My mom said so. And so did yours. I was watching cartoons but I was really listening to them talking. Don't worry, though," she put her arm around my shoulder. "Friends don't get adopterated and we are already friends. And," she stood back and held up her pointer finger, "you can only get adopterated one time so you're safe now. Your mom can't change her mind and send you back. There are rules." She smiled, glad to offer what she considered comforting news.

"If you're so sure I was adopterated, then when did it happen? Why didn't I know about it?"

"I told you—when you were a baby. Your mom even said she felt like she got away with something. She said you were like the prize at the County Fair, and she hit the bull's eye or something."

"What's a County Fair?" Wendy asked.

"Didn't you ever notice you have black hair and your parents have light brown hair? And your eyes are blue, but your parents' eyes are brown! My mom noticed and she asked your mom where you got your black hair and blue eyes and your mom said no one knows because you were adopterated." Tracy apparently understood the entire process, backing up her claim with genetic science, but I was more confused than ever.

"If I was adopterated," I asked Tracy, "how come my parents didn't tell me? You can't go around adopterating babies and not tell them."

"That's what your mom asked my mom: when should I tell Daphne? And my mom said to tell you soon or you'd figure it out on your own."

I remember feeling suddenly peculiar, like my head was packed with cotton. I kept shaking my head but this new knowledge wouldn't come loose, an anomaly wedged in between the blocks of what I'd thought was truth. Like a page thrust into a book between two pages I'd already read and memorized, this new page changed everything and contained information that disproved my accepted history.

I decided to give my parents one chance to come clean. They'd always taught me to tell the truth, and this was my opportunity to see if they followed their own rule. The dinner table would be the stage, and I would wait until they quizzed me about my day, then I'd turn the table on them (the dining table! I thought giddily).

"How was school today, Sweetie?" asked Mom.

"Fine," I gave my stock answer. "Someone asked me a question, and I didn't know the answer." I looked first at Dad, then at Mom. They appeared relaxed and happy. Unsuspecting.

"What was the question?" Dad finally asked.

"Who asked the question?" Mom asked at the same time.

"The question was," I sat up straighter to prepare myself and carefully watched both of their faces, "how does a child with blue eyes have two parents with brown eyes?" I gazed deep into both sets of brown eyes, searching for answers.

"Who asked you that?"

"Tracy. She heard you talking to her mom the other day."

"Well, it *is* scientifically possible for two brown-eyed parents to have a blue-eyed child, if each brown-eyed parent has a recessive blue-eyed gene," said Dad, "but we don't know for sure if that's the case with our family. We have a special case."

Before I could stop myself, I blurted, "Is this the part where you tell me I was adopterated?" My parents' laughter, loud and full, assaulted my ears. My face flushed and my heart felt like a raw chestnut, hard and tight, a potential choking hazard.

"Oh, Honey," Mom finally said, wiping her eyes and coming around the table to hug me.

"You've almost got it right," grinned Dad. "You were *adopted.* What this means is, um...Glory, tell our young lady what it means to be adopted."

"We've been wondering when and how to tell you about this," Mom started. Her eyes were big and wet.

"We're sorry you had to hear it on the playground first. That isn't fair," said Dad. "We should have told you before. We just didn't want you to feel...different. You know, about our family and belonging to us."

"Being adopted is very special," said Mom. "It's cool, you know, because we hoped and hoped for a baby, and we planned and wished and dreamed. Every seed we planted, we said to ourselves: when this flower blooms, we'll have a baby. Or, maybe our new baby will eat the vegetables from this seed."

"We must have planted and cultivated a thousand wishes and a million hopes," said Dad.

"And then one day, after our hope muscles were severely strained from so much use, we got a magic phone call."

"What's a magic phone call?" I asked.

"It's just like a regular phone call, but it brings news that your biggest hopes have been granted."

"I nearly fainted after that call," said Mom, "and we met you the next day."

They told me what little they knew about my birth mother, a girl still in high school who couldn't raise me, and how I fit so perfectly into the Hallorhan family they and all of our other relatives frequently forgot I didn't share their genes.

"You belong to us," said Dad. "You're part of our family."

Exhausted from my life story rewrite, I slept

soundly that night. The next morning the first thing I noticed was the sun, shining through my window like nothing had changed. The second thing I noticed was my new, as yet unfamiliar feeling of being a daisy in a bed of roses.

~~~

I've never considered the impact being adopted might have had on my fundamental personality. Sure, I liked to envision my 'real' family, a family with a me-sized hole in it, sitting down for dinner with a conspicuously empty chair, traveling with a vacant space in the car.

At first glance, I appear to be an average woman: 5'4" average height, blue eyes, jet black hair, fair skinned, well-adjusted and conservatively dressed. In reality, I'm a thirty-four year-old unemployed architect who lives with her mother. Every boyfriend I've ever had was unavailable for reasons ranging from geography to philosophy to marriage (his). I suffer from an affliction I call Identity Nebula and, like a plant without a category, I could be a perennial or an annual, wild or tame. I've been abandoned on foreign soil, forced to adapt to my new
~~~

environment or face extinction.

I became an architect to spite my parents, who own a landscaping business they'd hoped I'd happily inherit. Architects are more polished and professional than gardeners; they don't have dirty fingernails or garden clogs that squish with every step. Architects don't drive dented vans.

"Unless they're unemployed," I murmured aloud, startling myself.

As I stood in my boss's office accepting my termination, she blathered something about a layoff, saying I'm not being fired, but we both knew this was a permanent decision and semantics couldn't change the facts. My face wore a mannequin's expression to match my stiff posture while her words bounced off my plastic exterior. I imagined the words in their physical form ricocheting off me, returning to their speaker like sharp, pointy boomerangs to pierce her cool confidence, tearing her suit and bruising her face.

I've proudly displayed the title of architect for the last five years, tacking it onto the end of my name in even the least formal social situations, such as meeting friends of friends at backyard barbecues. "Hello, I'm Daphne Hallorhan, Architect," I'd say, extending my hand. It anchored me, this title, assuring I wouldn't drift away on a wave of anonymity, and I landed more than one client at casual gatherings with my simple announcement.

What will I say now? I wondered, robotically corralling my personal effects into an empty file box. Will I say, Hello, I'm Daphne Hallorhan, Unemployed Architect? No; too defeatist. Former Architect? No; too final. Can I still be an architect when I'm not actively working as an architect? I'm still licensed and I have a client roster, a network of decorators and real estate agents, landscape designers and lawn maintenance companies, temporary maid services and event coordinators. I eyed up my Rolodex, wondering if I was expected to leave it behind. I tucked it underneath my framed Frank Lloyd Wright sketch, wedging my coffee cup next to it to keep the tabs from getting crushed.

I grabbed the leather brief bag containing my field tools and portfolio, shoving a handful of business cards into the outer pocket. My work boots still sported gobs of mud from the job site I visited yesterday; I'd have to carry them separately. The file I'd built on that particular job rested in my work-in-progress tray, its contents neatly bound into the metal clip, a concise journal of the effort expended and my interpretation of the client's design style and expectations. I forced my gaze away from the file to prevent myself from taking it, knowing the guilt of absconding with company property would far outweigh the temporary satisfaction of petty retaliation.

This layoff, unwelcome and heart wrenching, is not a surprise. It's foolish to assume the slumping economy won't negatively impact jobs such as mine, as one of the first trends to occur in a depression (even if it's just a repression, like the grinning news anchors would have us believe) is mortgage defaults and bankruptcy filings. After the bankruptcies have time to settle and people are ready to move into a new house, they shop for modulars. Residential architecture is less and less in demand, unless one is interested in designing modular homes or apartment buildings. My work load has decreased steadily over the past two years, as even those who could afford a professional residential designer are opting to stay put until the economy recovers.

I'm so tired of the word economy I hope I never hear it again.

The desk phone rang, displaying my mother's number. "Hello?" I heard the waver in my voice and hoped she wouldn't detect it.

"Hi, Daphne," she said, "this is your mother

speaking." I smiled, the knot of disappointment loosening a notch. She always makes this announcement when she calls and my reaction varies from frustration to laughter, depending on my mood.

"What's up?" I tried to match her casual tone.

"Are you still coming over for dinner tonight?" I'd forgotten about our dinner plans, but dining alone seemed desolate. "I need you to pick up some hamburger. We've got an old friend of mine joining us."

"Oh, sure, no problem," I gave my stock answer, recognizing the presence of a third person as sufficient reason to postpone revealing my jobless status. My mother won't agree with my logic, but I'm loathe to share private details with people I've just met. Burdening someone with bad news moments after making their acquaintance feels like taking advantage somehow. Nice to meet you; please carry this for me. Not to mention, I don't want to be remembered as 'that girl who lost her job'. "I met someone today," the story will go, "an architect who just lost her job. Can you imagine? How will she find a similar position? It's tragic, really." The only tragedy here is allowing an incident to define one's identity.

<div style="text-align:center">~~~</div>

In typical Gloria Hallorhan fashion, my mother wasted no more than three seconds commiserating about my job loss before presenting the silver lining.

"Oh, honey, that's tragic, really tragic," she began, unaware she echoed the response I'd given the imaginary stranger. "But you know, the timing couldn't be more perfect. I just signed a client who wants a pretty complex landscape design, and I could really use your help on this project."

"I don't know if I'm ready for that yet. I just cleaned out my office and haven't had a chance to absorb the news, let alone plan my next move beyond submitting my resume everywhere. Well, everywhere around Madison. I don't want to apply to Chicago companies unless I get hungry."

"Chicago!" Her hand fluttered to her chest. "That's a bit extreme, don't you think? Why, you can make a perfectly comfortable living right here, working for Outer Peace. The company supported the three of us for decades and we never wanted for work. In fact, I'm thinking about selling it; you can have first dibs," her hand found my arm, a light yet comforting touch.

"Oh, Mom, I don't know," I hedged. "I'm an architect, not a landscape designer; I only took one class in college about landscapes. And I don't really know anything about running a company."

She waved my words away like they were insects with the potential to sting. "Nonsense, I can teach you that part. You have style, and you forge personal connections with your clients. You can envision their vision and make it happen, and that's what keeps a company running. And landscape design is related to architecture, you know. Think of it as outdoor architecture. You can be Nature's Architect!"

"You get a gold star for enthusiasm," I told her, grinning. It was impossible to maintain any level of negativity in the face of her ebullience. "Show me the project, and if I think I can do it, I'll give it my best shot."

"Your best shot will be a bull's eye," she said with a cheesy grin.

~~~

The project consisted of a Wright-style building featuring square shapes and simple lines, but the
~~~

surrounding yard hadn't yet recovered from construction. Spartan and flat, it begged for flora and foliage, color and texture. The answers on the client questionnaire helped shape a loose image of the finished product in my mind. The building, intended to be a dentist's office on one side and a spa on the other side, should appear to grow up out of the surrounding land. The grounds should be low maintenance and feature various pathways, sitting areas, and plantings, all designed to invoke a Zen-like calm for their clientele. The windows through which the dentists' patients would gaze while their cavities were filled should contain thick leaves and mature trees, an attempt to bring nature's serenity inside. If one were sitting on the spa side enjoying a pedicure or massage, one should view a private garden with a sitting bench or cozy conversation area. A water fountain or lazy looped stream was also on their list of requests.

My sketch took shape quickly. This challenge was exactly what I needed; I ignored my displeasure at my mother being right again, and immersed myself in the process. My knowledge of plants and their various needs is severely limited, as I've worked all my life to learn as little as possible about my parents' profession, afraid someday I'd be right where I am now, working for the family company.

After sketching the grounds and an aerial view of the proposed gardens, I created a spreadsheet and started inserting plants into every category I could think of: perennials, annuals, shade plants, sun plants, rocky soil tolerant, sandy soil tolerant, drought tolerant, preferred fertilizers, water requirements, leaf shape, leaf color, and for the flowering plants, bloom color and bloom schedule. I only included plants suggested for our specific climate zone, but I still ended up with a selection of over 300 plants.

A week had passed before I realized how consumed I was by this project, but I enjoyed the therapy-like benefits of creative design and the additional research afforded me an opportunity to connect with Mom on her turf. We sat together for hours discussing ground slope and plant placement, construction requirements for lazy loop streams and walkway curve calculations and seating placement. One debate centered on leaves: spiky vs. oval, dark vs. pale, shiny vs. dull. I'm not sure how many other projects Mom monitored while I struggled with this one, but she kept the spotlight trained on my progress as if it were her only assignment.

Twenty-three days after Mom handed me the file, I

returned it to her, four times as thick and containing a project portfolio ready for the client presentation. There were two plans included, each one incorporating all of the desired features listed on their client questionnaire. I'd designed a place I'd like to visit, envisioning myself beginning with a teeth cleaning and ending with a pedicure, enjoying the peaceful garden between appointments.

Mom would present the designs while I returned my BMW to the dealer, my lease up and my current salary unable to support such extravagance. I'd already moved into Mom's spare room when my apartment lease had ended, terrified I'd be unable to afford the rent for another year with no job prospect in sight.

In my mind the economy had adopted a grim reaper persona, following me with a steady, menacing gate, hacking away my lifestyle one luxury at a time. I survived by staying one pace ahead.

~~~

Like most things in life, when I finally got what I wanted—the thing that kept me up at night and blurred my focus during the day, the thing I'd harangued my
~~~

mother about since she'd revealed the presence of a family secret—the glory of victory was tinged with mild disappointment, fervent anticipation once again overshadowing the goal attainment. I can't imagine not wanting to know something; my curiosity is like an infinite pool, impossible to fill to a satisfactory level. My brain manages to turn every bit of knowledge I gain into a question, a quest for more, a visceral need to understand how, why, where, when, what next.

I probably should have been a journalist. As a journalist I'd have thrived. I would have pursued each story with the same single-minded, dogged persistence evident in my obsessive hunt for clues about my family tree. A simple fill-in the blank exercise for most people, at least for the closest two or three generations, ended up creating more questions than answers. Instead of a family tree, the depiction of my known lineage resembled a broken twig.

I stared at the hard won document clutched in my hand, wondering how much it had cost Mom to give it to me. Resisting my pleas must have been harder for her after Dad passed, but she'd managed for ten years until this final capitulation.

"I found it a few months ago when I cleaned out

the attic," she said quietly, "and I decided it was time to help you find your birth parents." She stood in the doorway, a slight figure, fragile in her nightgown with still-sleepy eyes and a pillow crease along one cheek.

"Thanks, Mom," I whispered. My face heated as I remembered various times I'd nagged, cajoled, urged and badgered her over the years.

We'd argued the night before as I blamed my insatiable curiosity for creating this fixation; I love my mother, I wouldn't have changed a thing about my childhood, but I want to know—I *need* to know—who my birth parents were and why they gave me up.

Ever since Tracy MacArthur's crash course in biology, my black hair and blue eyes have felt like banners announcing I didn't inherit any physical traits from Dean and Gloria Hallorhan, two brown-eyed blondes with long legs, confident in the knowledge of their identities.

"They were young," Mom always said of my birth parents. "It was a different time then. In 1975, you couldn't just have a baby and stay in high school and keep the baby and raise it. People frowned." She paused, remembering, "Your father and I tried and tried, and we couldn't get pregnant to save our lives. He can pollinate apple trees and roses all day long, but...well. Anyway, we were at a block party—they were all the rage here in the 70's—and someone there was planning to adopt a baby. They had different reasons than we did, they were more concerned about overpopulating the planet and saving an unwanted child, but we just wanted a family." This is when she'd gaze at me fondly and tap her fingertips on the table. She always cut her nails short in an effort to keep them clean and prevent them from tearing off while working.

"So, you managed to curb overpopulation, convert an unwanted child to a wanted one, and have a family all at once."

"Yes!" She chose to ignore my snide sarcasm, grinning and opening her arms like a priest addressing his congregation. "You came into our lives and we created our own microcosm right here, just the three of us, snug as bugs."

"And it was a closed adoption, but you buttered up the secretary and finagled a copy of my real birth certificate," I steered her back to the reality of facts and paperwork. This usually deflated her a bit, and I always felt a twinge of shame. The twinge was weak, though; not enough to prevent me from plowing forward.

"Well, I didn't butter her up, exactly. We became

friends. Her name was Suzie and she was so organized it was inspiring. And back then, believe it or not, I had curiosity like yours," her expression begged for understanding, but I wasn't buying. "I only had to ask her once, the last time we visited her office to collect the final paperwork, and she whipped out that piece of paper so fast I thought later she must have planned to give it to me anyway."

It seemed odd to read an official document containing vital information about people related to me, whom I'd never met. The name on the birth certificate, Daisy Faye Harrison, sounded whimsical and flimsy.

I stared at my parents' names and the names stared back at me. Harold Bartholomew (a dash indicated he had no middle name) and Marcia Audrey Harrison. The names kept their secrets well hidden, sufficiently generic, imparting no clue regarding ancestry, personality or religion. Pedestrian names. Stoic names. The names squatted in awkward comfort on the lines, a stubborn claim of space, evoking no friendly gestures or goodwill. Marcia and Harold could be lawyers or bums. Or both.

The twig of my family tree has nascent roots.

My curiosity is a motivational tool, but also a handicap. I've learned to allow my imagination to conjure possibilities, ideas, theories and fictions from facts in an attempt to consider all plausible and implausible angles before seeking the answer to my next question. I've found a cooling period of three days sufficient for my genealogy project, so every time I find a new piece of information, I allow my curiosity the short-lived satisfaction of another puzzle piece slipping into place while I let my imagination scurry through all possible implications. This process is my way of diverting disappointment in the next puzzle piece, and preventing (hopefully) any impetuous actions I would later regret. So far, it's working. It's feeding my obsessive compulsive tendencies, but I'll worry about that later. Right now I'm making those tendencies work for me.

~~~

Memories of my childhood are always accompanied by a sense of shame. Dramatic, I know, and typical of any human who survives to adulthood. I always felt mine was a unique suffering, though: not only did my status as an unwanted baby grant me automatic social dorkitude, but the complete lameness, the decidedly un-hipness, of my adoptive parents guaranteed I'd make
~~~

the Nerd Hall of Fame. Mine were the only parents in all of Central Elementary School who made a living digging in the dirt, and they actually *worked* for some of my classmates' parents or the companies where those parents worked. Essentially, they grew up but never left the sand box.

Our vehicles were always pick-up trucks or panel vans. Profound embarrassment! My classmates would glide up to the sidewalk in front of the school in chic, smooth cars, the briefly gaping door allowing a peek of a perfectly coiffed mother or father in respectable business attire. My arrival, on the other hand, was heralded by the distinctive clanking of shovels and rakes suspended from the primitive ladder rack Dad designed and fabricated. Unless the truck was less than a year old, an interesting pattern of dents and scratches decorated the tailgate and I'd have to perform an acrobatic jump when exiting to fully clear the truck without suffering a smear of mud on my clean, but wrinkled, clothes.

My parents always wore shorts or cargo pants, preferring the various pockets to using a tool belt. One boy at school once asked me if my parents went on safaris all the time. It sounds petty, I know, but these details attract cruel comments from the self-proclaimed cool kids like crows on a fresh carcass.

No, I wouldn't trade the parents who found and raised me even if I could. I simply wondered if my biological mother resembled one of those TV-perfect parents glimpsed through the other kids' car doors.

~~~

Harold and Marcia climbed into my head and made themselves comfortable, keeping me up at night and distracting me during the day. They refused to remain in the corner of my room, where the genealogy bulletin board and files are kept. Every time I started the computer I searched for all variations of their names, learning irrelevant facts about men named Harry Bartholomew who coached Little League in Texas or won marathons in Connecticut. They were all way too old or way too young to be my father. I wondered if he was a lawyer, policeman, fireman, teacher or engineer. I hoped he was kind and had a sense of humor. I hoped his regrets invaded his sleep.

Marcia's name was more popular than Harold's. I searched for her maiden name, since that was all I knew for sure, and found fifty-nine Marcia Harrisons, some
~~~

with an additional surname and some without, in the USA. After eliminating the ones whose married names were Harrison and the ones who were way too old or too young to be my mother, I was left with eight possibilities. Of these, I found photo profiles that helped me remove one black woman and two swarthy, black-haired women from my list. I created a matrix with all of the information I'd found so far, ranking the remaining contenders in geographical order, closest to farthest, since this was the most economical approach. Three of the five Marcia Harrisons lived within driving distance of my place in Madison; the other two lived in Texas and Oklahoma. I couldn't really imagine living in such dry, dusty places.

Name	Age	Occupation	Location
Marcia A. (Harrison) Miller	50	attorney	Chicago, IL
Marcia A. Harrison	50	civil engineer	Ottumwa, IA
Marcia A. (Harrison) Millinen	49	bookstore owner	Iron Falls, MI
Marcia (Harrison) Zykowski	49	interior designer	Broken Arrow, OK

Marcia A. (Harrison) Vigmostad	51	waitress	San Antonio, TX

I studied the graph, considering each possible candidate as objectively as possible given the limited information. Marcia Miller was easy to imagine: my mind's eye created a slim woman in an expensive business suit and pumps, moving with athletic economy and practicality, working in a high-rise, wearing her hair at a sensible length. I'm certain she drove a smooth riding car in an appropriately executive shade of gray.

The second name on my list conjured a less elegant woman with a singular focus. Still a spinster, she most likely lived and breathed work, spending her idle hours contemplating the tensile strength of steel. The third Marcia, a married business owner, is bookish, probably easily distracted and wears decorative scarves. She's married, probably wrote her own vows, and probably agonizes over wording while holding regular conversations. The interior designer in Broken Arrow sounded depressing to me; although, beautifying the inside of houses and public spaces might trick citizens into more easily tolerating the featureless landscapes of Oklahoma. I shook my head, chuckling at my own distaste for the Great Plains with their treeless, endless horizon. Marcia Vigmostad, like the Marcia in Oklahoma, must spend most of her time spelling her last name, and the word 'waitress' immediately inserted an image into my mind's eye of Flo snapping her gum in Mel's Diner and telling the customers to kiss her grits. I hoped she worked as a waitress for something to do, not because she needed the money and had no other skills.

Marcia Millinen's location caught my eye: Michigan. I reached for my birth certificate and confirmed she'd listed Madison as her address, but Michigan was her birthplace. Harold was born there as well. Was it possible she'd only lived in Madison briefly, and moved back to her home state? A computer search revealed Agate County's courthouse document retrieval system, but I had to be directly related to the person in question to request a birth certificate. The site contained a link to tax rolls, which I selected, eagerly typing 'Harrison' in the search box.

My eyes dry and my neck rigid, I took a deep breath and sought a mini-meditation like our local Yoga instructor often promoted. Yoga wasn't really my style, but it made me feel refreshed and elastic and somehow more capable in a fairly efficient fashion. I forced myself to attend the classes three times a week and performed my own sun salutation every morning before I stepped into the shower, reveling in the effects of deep breathing and simple stretching.

The database finally relinquished a short list of Harrison-owned property descriptions. There weren't as many Harrisons as I'd expected—they all fit on one page, a neat list of five entries. The town names where they owned property were strangely beckoning: Houghton, Gogebic, Hastings Junction, Ontonagon. I printed it out and started my next search: Millinen. The results appeared faster for this second search, the virtual secretary apparently in full document retrieval mode. There was only one entry: Millinen, Evan and Marcia, husband and wife. They lived in Iron Falls, Michigan. I gulped and printed out this page as well, adding it to the file I'd created.

Over the years I've set many deadlines for locating my birth parents. My poor mother had to explain the adoption process to me a few times before I finally understood and accepted her claim: her blood did not flow through my veins; I didn't *really* have my father's nose; and I hadn't inherited my proclivity for reading and other solitary pursuits from my maternal grandmother. Unless, of course, my biological (a difficult word to pronounce for a seven-year-old) relatives had these same traits and interests. My initial reaction had been numbed disbelief followed quickly by a panicked identity crisis, followed just as quickly by a vow to "locate my birth parents before my tenth birthday". Ten had seemed so far away at the time, I was confident I'd solve the riddle before then, and with minimal effort.

Since then, I've consciously set this project aside in order to finish high school, then college, start a career and establish myself. I'd wanted to be an architect ever since I first realized someone actually received money for designing houses and offices and I wouldn't have to dirty my hands to make a living. My interest is in clean, efficient design (it's even part of my tagline, appearing on my business card and website) and my client roster is usually full. That is, it was full before my termination.

Over the years my emotions regarding my birth mother have changed from anger toward the ungrateful, irresponsible mother who abandoned me to a kind of forgiveness—an understanding of sorts that maybe it was a case of wrong place, wrong time. Then I wondered how my birth parents would react when I finally tracked them down and announced my identity: jubilation? Disinterest? Denial? Despair? This line of thinking would cripple my ambition and halt my momentum.

This time, though, was different. I would allow no rogue disparaging thoughts to derail me, entertaining only positive ideas and maintaining focus on the daunting, ever-narrowing time line.

~ ~ ~

I packed four times for my sojourn to the UP, designing a complete wardrobe each time and then rejecting each outfit before zipping the suitcase shut. I finally settled on the simplest pieces with the least color.

The two lane highway stretched before me, each side flanked by crowded trees, nearly hypnotizing in its sameness. I pulled over to check the map, afraid to rely on the GPS in my car in this rural, barren area. How could highway miles take so long to traverse? I saw three cars within one hour and wondered where they were all going. Were they on similar goose chases?

Marcia Millinen's book store website featured a bio page that mentioned her childhood in Hastings Junction.

It listed cheerleading and reading as her two favorite high school activities, and mentioned her degree in Creative Writing from Northern Michigan University. This brief personal history inspired me to consult a map and plan a road trip, taking a long weekend to forget about my current situation. Visiting Hastings Junction before exploring Marcia's current location in Iron Falls would give me a chance to see where she'd grown up while allowing me time to explore the UP and legitimately postpone our meeting. Now that our meeting was closer, the thought of our first encounter became more and more terrifying. So far the trip seemed an exercise in busyness, a made-up distraction designed to trick myself into thinking I was making progress on the search. I kept expecting to see a goose's tail feathers disappearing around the next gentle bend in the highway.

This is a fact-finding mission, I reminded myself under my breath. *It's a reconnaissance.* The slim file I'd created lay on the front passenger seat next to the camera and Moleskine notebook. I wished for a set of spy tools ala James Bond so I could covertly record conversations and snap photos by tapping a button on my watch, but I'd have to settle for my iPhone recorder if it came to that.

I wondered how I'd be received if I walked into

Marcia's bookstore and announced my identity. Would Marcia think my appearance was the next logical chapter in her life? Would she be horrified to learn who I was? *I don't even know if she's the right one yet*, I reminded myself. I was following my gut instinct, something I said I'd never do. My natural inclination included logical, deductive reasoning, lists, weighted considerations of various possibilities or outcomes. I only enjoyed spontaneity when it was scheduled; I didn't like surprises, even good ones, and impetuous actions were so rare for me I can count on one hand the times I've committed them. Part of my acclimation to joblessness, it seemed, consisted of spontaneity exercises.

The sign welcoming me to Hastings Junction (population 313) jarred me out of my reverie and forced me to pay attention. This was the first intersection I'd encountered in the last fifty miles or so, and I shot beneath the blinker light and out the other side of town before I realized I'd just driven through it. I turned around in the next driveway and approached the intersection at a more sedate speed, this time noticing the main street was perpendicular to the highway I traveled.

I turned down the main street—the only street intersecting with the highway—trying to imagine living here, wondering how far off the highway the residential streets looped and strayed. The image on Google Maps had resembled a small crosshatch pattern with a few tendrils reaching out in lazy coils, all of it situated in a seemingly random location surrounded by trees. The town presented a forlorn facade, one foot still mired in the slow demise of winter and the other foot not quite yet landed in the fresh bloom of spring.

My reservation for the night was at Hannah's, a mom and pop establishment judging from the way they answered the phone. "Hiya," she'd said.

"Um...hello. Is this Hannah's Cabins?" I double-checked the phone number I'd dialed while I waited for her answer.

"You betcha! You lookin' for a reservation, honey?"

"Yes, I'd like one room please, or one small cabin, for the night of May 15th, if you have any vacancies then."

"Oh lordy, we have vacancies all the way up to tourist season, which starts with a bang on Memorial Day weekend! You oughta see it. It's like all the tourists are waiting to hear a gunshot go off so's they can spring on up here and invade our—" she sighed abruptly, apparently remembering that she was talking to a tourist right now. "Anyway, I'll give you the cutest little cabin we've got. Just you wait til you see it, honey. You're gonna love it."

"Okay, great. Thank you. Do you need a credit card to hold the reservation for me?"

"Oh honey, we don't take credit cards. We take cash or personal checks. I don't tell everyone we take personal checks, but I can tell from your voice that you're honest so I'll take yours. Don't worry, your name is in the book. I'll hold it open for ya. Not that anyone else is gonna be lookin' for a room that night anyway, but I wrote you down just to be sure. You comin' from a long ways away?"

"Huh? Oh, I'm coming from Madison, Wisconsin."

"Wah! That's eight hours away. If the traffic is movin' along, that is. Drive safely honey, and I'll see you soon."

Hannah's, it turned out, was situated at the end of the main street two blocks from the grocery store and next door to the Hasty Pub. It looked like a residence with a small, hand-lettered sign next to the door announcing 'Hannah's Cabins'. There was no parking lot, so I pulled over near the curb and knocked on the front door.

Hannah looked just as I expected: curly bottle-blonde hair, Capri pants and gum she snapped incessantly. Her age was difficult to judge. I guessed she was somewhere between forty and sixty-five.

"Daphne!" She chirped, arms spread in welcome, as if I were here favorite high school classmate here for the reunion.

"You must be Hannah," I offered my hand to shake.

"Oh, you are cute as a button. Come here, honey," she gathered me in for a quick lilac-scented hug. I felt like I was greeting a favorite aunt after a prolonged absence.

The cabins sat behind the house, a tangle of footpaths linking them to each other and to the main house. I pulled my car around the block into the alley to park near the first cabin. Each cabin featured a different animal on the door to identify it from the others; I was sleeping in the Moose cabin tonight. Hannah assured me it was the most 'female friendly' cabin by virtue of its larger bathroom and pink and brown bedspread.

"If you're hungry, or lonely, or feel like mingling, pop on over to the Hasty Pub next door here," she said, gesturing with her left hand. "They have good food and there're always lots of people around."

I paced around the cabin, nearly bumping into myself. *Clearly*, I thought, *I can't settle down and rest right now.* A glance at my phone confirmed the time (7:00) and the poor cell signal (one bar). I texted my mom to let her know I arrived, freshened my makeup and added a scarf to dress up my t-shirt and jean jacket for my solo dinner at the Pub.

Eating alone is one of my favorite ways to enjoy a meal in Madison; I eat alone more often than I eat with someone, frequently taking my laptop to a coffee shop or cafe and working on my current files. There are fewer interruptions in a public restaurant than there are at my desk, and sometimes I end up staying two or three hours while I work through a problem. I'll miss the restaurants, now that I'm unemployed. I've found some of my most creative solutions to dimension or angle issues while munching on salad or pie and sipping tepid coffee. Entering a bar alone in a small town where I know no one, however, isn't quite as relaxing.

The minute I swung the door open and stepped inside the dim room, all noise ceased as the patrons at the bar rotated their heads in one syncopated movement to see who'd entered. The bartender smiled a welcome as the customers all turned their heads back to study the wall behind the bar and resume their conversations. Nodding at the bartender, I glanced about quickly and chose a small table along the wall near the juke box where I'd be able to observe everyone and hopefully get a feel for the town by learning about its citizens. Or at least the citizens who gathered at the Hasty Pub on a Friday night. I wondered if this group represented a large demographic sample or a small one.

"You must be the one driving the car with Wisconsin plates. Welcome to Hastings Junction!" The bartender grinned and offered me a menu.

"Wow, you notice everything around here. I've only been in town for about thirty minutes!" I smiled to soften my tone.

"Well, it ain't much of a challenge to notice strangers stopping in here before Memorial Day. It's not like we get any tourists or anything until then. Whatcha like to drink?"

"You know, it's been a long day," I told her. "I'd really like a dirty martini. With Stoli, if you have it. I also need to eat, so I'll place a food order as well."

"A dirty martini, ay? Funny, I just learned how to make those yesterday and now you're the fourth person to order one. You'll be the first with Stoli, though. That costs an extra 50 cents, just so you know." She looked like she still attended high school, long and lean and confident.   Maybe it was her pony tail and clear complexion that made her appear so youthful.   I wondered if this bar was a family business owned by her parents or grandparents.

"That's fine," I smiled at her.   She was already bopping back behind the bar and reaching for the bottle of Stoli.   The menu was short and simple.   Everything was deep fried or cooked on the grill. I generally avoided fried foods and dreaded the stomachache I knew would assault me in a couple hours, but in an effort to experience the local culture, I ordered French fries and a veggie burger with mushrooms and Swiss cheese when the bartender delivered my martini.

"Holy wah!" exclaimed the bartender, startling me. "That's hilarious!   No, seriously, what would you like to order?"   Her pen was poised over the order pad.   She finally glanced at my face and must have seen my confusion. "We don't have veggie burgers.   They're all made from beef."

"Oh..."   I said, "in that case, I'll have the French fries and a grilled cheese sandwich."   I shuddered, thinking of ingesting grease and gelatinous cheese. On white bread! I'd have to do some extra push-ups to pay for this. The bartender grabbed the menu and carried it back to the bar, holding it high in one hand with a triumphant posture.

A few more people trickled through the door, tired parents with toddlers and young kids who shrieked and chased each other around the pool table. "Where's Delores Hastings?" yelled one little boy, racing to one of the bar stools and pulling a man's pant leg. "Mr. Brown? Where's Delores Hastings?"

Mr. Brown slowly swiveled his head to study the boy. "Hi, Petey. Delores Hastings is around here somewhere. Maybe she's hiding under the pool table." The boy ran off, presumably in search of Ms. Hastings, just as I felt something nudge my leg.

A large chocolate lab with liquid brown eyes stared back at me with an expression cultivated specifically for coercing me into petting her. The children all bounded up in a group, exclaiming, "Delores Hastings! We found you, girl!" and they all tried to pet her at once.

"Is this your dog?" I asked the boy named Petey.

"No, silly!" Petey laughed. "Delores Hastings lives here at the bar." He shook his head as if he wondered how in the world I didn't know this.

"She...lives here?" I asked. Delores, for her part, patiently tolerated the pets and tugs from the kids, sitting still with a prim, straight face. The only indication she enjoyed this attention was her tail, thumping on the floor.

"Well, yeah," said Petey, slapping his forehead with a palm. "She's Mr. Brown's dog, and he owns the bar."

"She's a bar slut," said another boy, proud to share his knowledge.

"Michael, didn't your parents tell you not to say that?" asked Petey, sounding like a hall monitor.

"Well, it's true. Mr. Brown calls her a bar slut all the time," said Michael, grinning at me.

"I think it's supposed to be a joke, Michael," Petey explained. "It's a grown-up joke and we aren't supposed to say it."

"Where did she get the name Delores Hastings? Is she named after a person?" I asked.

"Yep, the real Delores Hastings was the mayor's wife or something. When our town was just a baby," said Petey. One of the parents suddenly realized the children were talking to someone they didn't know, and the kids were all summoned to their tables to eat. Delores Hastings eased herself to the floor and rested her head on my feet.

The parents monitored me from the corners of their eyes, nodding curtly in my direction when I glanced around the room. If it weren't for Delores Hastings I would feel snubbed. The waitress spoke with forced friendliness, her jaw clenching as she asked me if I needed another drink. Pretty soon a few more people sauntered through the door, greeting everyone in turn as they were greeted by everyone, their eyes lingering on my face for a moment before resuming their visual sweep.

Snippets of conversation drifted my way, disjointed bits of discourse including advice on how to pass a breathalyzer (gargle with WD-40), why Eileen aka Cinderella insisted on drinking before her AA meetings (she was never gonna quit drinkin' anyhow, so why start just because a judge sent her to an AA meeting?), and a summary of Ida Mae's 99th birthday party fiasco (something involving an electric wheelchair and a prosthetic leg). I learned about the paternity of one Clay Crenshaw, a young man who had apparently died at a young age without his real father or the man he thought was his father ever knowing the truth. Except, apparently, for a group of people who'd witnessed the sensational performance of Clay's mother's best friend one night when she'd had a few drinks at home before proceeding to the bar and announcing the sordid secret to anyone who'd listen. Suddenly, my ears perked up as someone said the name Harrison.

"Did you hear about Mitch Harrison's award?" This was a man wearing a football jersey, facing away from me at the next table. I studied my plate, concentrating on my few remaining French fries.

"What? I thought he died, like a year ago," the bartender interrupted as she delivered a round of fresh beers. "He was so cute..."

"Yeah, he died in a car wreck. Then he got the lifetime achievement award from the State for solving crimes," another man said. He wore a t-shirt that read: I might be drunk, but you're ugly and I'll be sober in the morning. *Attractive*, I thought acidly.

"I think he solved every crime he ever worked on," said jersey guy. "Good for Mitchie, ya know. Too bad he isn't around to see it."

The name Mitch Harrison was familiar. Was he Marcia's dad? No, he would've retired a few years ago. The bartender had said he was cute, but I had no idea what her cuteness criteria consisted of. Maybe he was Marcia's brother; that made more sense.

The next day I drove through the streets of Hastings Junction, circling past the address I'd found in the tax roll for Mitchell and Faye Harrison (*that's* where I'd seen his name before!). They had owned this house since 1973, and I assumed they were Marcia's parents. I parked across the street from their house for a few moments and took a couple photos, feeling like a foolish female version of Columbo. Theirs was a neat, tidy yard tucked around a square house with a wide front porch. It was a story and a half. I envisioned Mitch (if there was a brother named Mitch) and Marcia's bedrooms in the upper level, ceilings slanting to hardwood floors and window seats inviting study sessions and cozy telephone chats with friends. Suddenly nervous someone would notice me, I pulled away from the curb and headed toward the grocery store to buy a snack for the ride to Iron Falls.

The Hastings IGA featured a slanting hardwood floor polished to a fierce shine, high ceilings and bright, well-stocked shelves. It had an air of bustle even though there were only two other customers trolling through the aisles. I grabbed a bag of chips (*why stop eating grease now?* I thought), an apple and a bottle of water and stood in line behind a man named Tommy, according to his shirt, with frayed long john sleeves flaring out at his wrists. His stubbled face looked kind as he nodded hello to me.

"Hey Tommy," said the cashier. "How'd you like those stuffed green peppers last night?"

"What?" He rubbed his jaw. "Oh yeah, for dinner. They were pretty good. You peeking in my windows again?"

She laughed. "No, silly, I was working when your wife stopped in here yesterday after work. I figured she was fixin' to make stuffed green peppers for dinner. I'm part detective, you know," the cashier winked at Tommy, a casual flirtation perfected by familiarity. She enjoyed this part of her job, I thought, the safety of flirting with people she knew, people who were married or otherwise engaged and posed no threat, no promise, no responsibility beyond that of brief entertainment.

"I guess you are, Tara," Tommy chuckled. "You have a good day, now," he said as he gathered up his purchases and walked toward the door. "Oh, you've got old Mrs. Pendergast pulling up out here. Want me to get her order for you?" A long, yellow Cadillac was pulling into the parking lot, gliding carefully into position in the space nearest the door.

Tara glanced out the front window. "Please, if you have time. If not, she'll wait for me." Tommy exited the store, stopping to greet Mrs. Pendergast. He came back into the store before Tara had finished ringing up my purchases.

"She needs cat litter, butter and hair spray," he called to Tara. "She says you know the kind she likes."

"Thanks Tommy, I'll take it from here. You take care, now," Tara smiled.

Tommy waved and left the store again. Suddenly feeling a bit left out, I asked Tara, "Can I help you with anything?"

"Um, no, but thank you. Mrs. Pendergast just has trouble getting in and out of her car, so we run the groceries out to her." Tara glanced toward the door, then back at me. "She's not even supposed to drive, you know, but she's a stubborn old thing. She's like ninety-nine or a hundred and one or something. She'll probably drive to her own funeral just to prove she can." She laughed. "Sorry, I just, like, really admire her, you know? She's a cool old lady. She's strong."

"She sounds like a grand old dame," I said, walking

toward the door as Tara wished me a good day.

In order to reach my car, I had to walk past Mrs. Pendergast's driver's side door. As I neared her car, a skeletal hand shot out and clutched my sleeve. "Say," she said, unaware how she'd startled me, "you look familiar." She looked me up and down, searching my face intently. "Do I know you, young lady?"

"I—I don't think so," I stammered, bending to return her gaze. She looked recently coiffed, though her lipstick strayed a bit to the left. We stayed frozen for a long beat while she searched her mental files and I waited. She clicked her dentures and let go of my arm.

"You remind me of a girl I once knew," she finally said. "A girl and her twin brother. They were rascals, always talking at the same time, finishing each other's sentences and telling each other's jokes," her eyes bore into mine. "You could be her daughter, if she had one," she grinned, turning toward Tara with a fistful of dollars to pay for the groceries Tara deposited in the back seat.

I backed up, turning slowly before jogging to my car. As I pulled out of the parking lot, Mrs. Pendergast waved her scarecrow's arm out the window and flashed me a sharp-eyed grin.

I spent the drive to Iron Falls wondering what it was like to grow up in a place like Hastings Junction where everyone knew everyone else, down to their lineage and their private habits. The safety of knowing everyone was looking out for you would be nice, I thought, but it seemed the constant intimacy would tire a person out. And the blatant, instinctual distrust of strangers! In Madison, I might not see anyone I knew for days and days unless I stopped in the office or met someone for lunch. I couldn't imagine going to a grocery store where the clerk already knew what I'd eaten for dinner the night before. On the other hand, the personal attendance for old Mrs. Pendergast would be hard to find in a city. She didn't even have to request special treatment here; it was automatically granted when she started having trouble walking.

How could a teenaged girl manage to get pregnant, carry the baby to term, give birth and put it up for adoption, all without anyone noticing? I thought.

Was I a skeleton in Marcia's closet?

~ ~ ~

When I was in college and meeting many new people, I would sometimes experience a wild, brief panic when I uttered my name, Daphne Hallorhan, this moniker bestowed by my adoptive parents, who had no real grip on who I was supposed to be. I felt insincere, tossing out this made-up name, even as I liked the name itself. I was the only Daphne I'd ever met and aside from Scooby-Doo references, had no preconceived images of how a Daphne might look or act.

Back then, I wondered what my real name would have been, if I'd been named and raised by my birth mother like a normal child, and I worried that my true biological identity, unknown to me, was somehow evident to others. At the time, I knew I was adopted and I realized no one in my family knew the birth family, so I could potentially be related to strangers on the street. I always searched for similar features in the faces of other college students, especially those a few years younger than I was, figuring my birth mother could have had another child on purpose a few years after she'd had me.

My favorite strategy for convincing people (and

myself) that my name really was Daphne Hallorhan, was to use a pseudonym as a sort of decoy when meeting someone. "Hello," a potential friend or roommate would say, hand extended. "I'm Tina."

"Hey there Tina," I'd respond. "My name is Myrtle."

"Oh...that's a nice name," fake smile, philosophical shrug.

"Actually," I'd grin, letting them in on my first joke as a new buddy/colleague/roommate. "It's Daphne. Daphne Hallorhan. Nice to meet you." This is when I'd manufacture my most sincere, welcoming smile, and grasp their hand to shake in a spirit of nascent camaraderie.

Girls usually maintained a modicum of poise when I used one of my old lady names, but boys regularly lost the battle between facial expression and social graces. One in particular stands out in my memory: a junior in college, two years ahead of me, broad-shouldered, square-jawed and leaking charisma from every pore, camouflaging his caveman-esque standard of etiquette. My roommate Tina was introducing us.

"Nathan, I want you to meet my roommate," said Tina, gesturing toward me.

"Bertha," I said, tilting my head and smiling.

Nathan flinched. "Really? That's your name?" *Smooth, Nate* I thought.

"No, it's Daphne. Daphne Hallorhan."

"Well, *that's* better! I was *hoping* you were jerking my chain!" He guffawed, slipping off my list of possible boyfriends with a whoosh. I almost heard it. "Does anyone ever call you Velma?"

"No." Was he trying to be witty?

Mom's capitulation (her term), when she gave me my original birth certificate, somehow opened the floor for more discussions about my adoption. Mom had all but met Marcia personally, she said, with Suzie acting as liaison between both parties for the adoption agency. Suzie liked both Marcia and Mom so much, she shared more than just Marcia's personal profile. She repeated conversations, enhanced in the telling by her own conjecture and interpretation.

After my first year of college, Mom broached the subject again, and answered the (unasked) name question for me.

"Marcia seems older than her years," Suzie had confided. "She thinks the baby is going to be a girl, and she seems fixated on the name Daisy." Suzie told Mom the worst part of her job was getting so close to people, helping them through one of the most trying times of their lives, then losing touch with them forever. She said she went through an abbreviated grieving process each time one of the babies was placed with adoptive parents, thereby terminating her purpose in their lives.

"I can't name her Daisy!" Mom had exclaimed. Daisies were weeds and she and Dad owned a landscaping business. What sort of message would that send to their clients? Anyone could grow weeds! "But what could I call you, that would honor our business? Violet? Too old lady. Marigold? Too nursery rhyme. Ivy? Ugh. Creeping Myrtle?" This last suggestion caused brief hysteria, and sometimes when I call home I announce myself as Creepy Myrtle calling. "And all I could think of," said Mom, seeing the distant past superimposed on the far wall, "was a young girl plucking the petals from a daisy and saying 'she lives' and 'she lives not', like she was deciding between abortion and adoption." Uncontrollable emotion betrayed Mom's usually stoic countenance for a few seconds, cracking her voice and turning her mouth down. She forced herself to brighten, taking a deep breath. "So, we named you Daphne. It's classier and has no botanical connotations. Your middle name, Dewdrop, we chose as a symbol of both nature and freshness—fresh as a daisy—without actually using the name Daisy."

~~~

There was no chance I'd blow through Iron Falls before realizing I'd entered it, as it has its own exit off the highway (anticipating future expansion?) and is situated on the edge of Lake Superior, offering a postcard-worthy view of village and water as I crossed the bridge spanning Iron Creek and observed the falls. The main street was lined with trees and flowers, the only moving thing a short parade of wagons and bikes heading down the wide sidewalk toward the corner store. A man on a riding lawnmower pulled out in front of me to dart toward the gas station, waving a hand in greeting, welcome or apology, or some combination of same. He had a cooler strapped on the back of his mower, which he opened now to swap an empty beer for a full one. I passed the gas station and continued to drive aimlessly, looping around residential blocks, admiring the old (mining boom?) houses and tidy yards, the brickwork and stonework and architectural details.

A sign reading 'Turn the Page' suddenly caught my
~~~

attention, swinging in the gentle breeze. I pulled over to study it. The letters were starting to peel, onion skin layers molting and flaking off. Paper flowers, crafted from the pages of books, hung suspended on filament above a miniature park bench with a blanket flung over the back of it. Stacks of books decorated the bench and the ground. A poster read *Participate in literary sport: read outside!* The vignette inspired in me a compulsion to enter the store and fill a couple of book bags with the latest novels; I envisioned myself leaving the store laden with tomes, ready to seek a quiet park where I could curl up under a tree and read until the leaves fell off next autumn.

My legs shook as I stepped on the sidewalk and I realized I'd quit breathing, my lungs locked and unable to accept air. I stumbled back to my car, entering the passenger door, to breathe and check my face in the mirror and reapply my lipstick. Thus fortified, I approached the store again while my mind maintained a frantic rhythm of doubts and suppositions. *Maybe she's not working today; maybe she has employees and she just manages the business; maybe she won't recognize me anyway; why would she? She can't be expecting me; she won't suspect my identity; I don't even know if we're related; I have to stop assuming we have a biological connection. I might look at her face and know it's her; I might not see any resemblance; how do I play this? Cool and detached? (Like I'm just a generic person passing through, secure in my knowledge of the circumstances of my birth.) Direct and courteous? (Like I'm here for the reason I'm really here, with a list of questions longer than I am tall, and a visceral need to know if she's the Marcia Harrison who gave up a baby girl for adoption in July 1975 and does she think of me? Does she have regrets? Does she wonder what happened to me or how our lives would have been different if she'd somehow been able to raise me herself?) Each* scenario was more terrifying than the last.

I pulled on the door three times, thinking it difficult to open, finally realizing the store was closed. A sigh of relief escaped me before I could consciously muster a reaction.

~~~

After a brief, silent debate with myself during which I nearly blacked out before realizing I'd once again suppressed my breath, I decided to check Marcia's house. I'd already come this far and devoted this much energy to my search, and I might as well take advantage of the altitude of my anxiety level, which allowed me to at least
~~~

appear courageous. I concentrated on driving, carefully stopping at each stop sign and accelerating slowly, enjoying the short cruise down the tree-lined, sun-dappled streets. I imagined Marcia traveling this route to and from the store each day. My actions felt vaguely illicit, as if I were embarking on my first stalking mission.

Finally arriving at the address I'd found on the tax rolls, I verified the house number three times, forward and backward, appreciating the palindromic numbers (1331) neatly arranged on the house. The two-story brick cape cod conjured images of children playing, fresh-baked bread, cozy hearth and family. The yard was neat, clearly designed for minimal upkeep with a gracefully curving line of bushes, some tulips and daffodils poking up through the earth between them.

Listening to my breath, I approached the house at a clip and banged the door knocker four times before stepping back to shut the storm door. No answer, and no sounds of activity inside. I repeated my knock and waited again. I glanced up and down the street: no action. *Maybe they're in the back yard*, I thought, trying to hide my window-peeking intention from myself. I circled the house, maintaining at least ten feet of space from the walls and calling out an occasional "hello" hoping a nosy neighbor wouldn't mistake me for a cat burglar.

As I neared the back corner of the house, I noticed a thin spiral of smoke across the yard. A tall, slim black-haired woman stood with her arms crossed, gazing down at the fire. She turned toward me as I approached her, our eyes taking in the familiarity of each other's faces. I held out my hand.

"My name is Daphne," My voice wavered. "I think we might be related."

She smiled and nodded, her cold hands grasping mine. "I was hoping you'd find me," she said.

Homecoming

1975

The boys played their hardest, for once following the coach's direction to the letter after each huddle, never flagging even when the rain started after the third quarter and quickly morphed the field from friendly lawn to revolting mud hole. In this Homecoming game, the Hastings Eagles were rounding out a stupendous season with twelve wins and one loss. They were determined to make this their lucky thirteenth win.

The score was tied at half-time: 14-14.

As always, two boys stood out on the team: the quarterback and the wide receiver, working in concert with well-choreographed throws and catches, dazzling the audience with their athleticism as the remaining teammates blended into the background, blocking the Timberwolves at every turn.

The crowd stood to watch the entire second half of the game, clapping along with the pep band and yelling encouragement to their team. No one seemed to notice the rain.

The score remained even.

Finally, near the end of the fourth quarter, the Eagles' quarterback aimed once more at a vacant area of the field and shot the ball like a missile, to be nabbed at the last moment by the wide receiver, the other team stumbling around. The wide receiver sprinted into the end zone before half of the other team realized where he'd gone, spiking the ball as the clock hit the last second.

The buzzer sounded and players and fans erupted onto the field, boosting the wide receiver and the quarterback onto their shoulders.

There's nothing better than a hometown football game on a Friday night. Especially a tidily won Homecoming game in a small, close-knit town.

The subsequent celebration, both an acknowledgement of a successful season and a sad farewell to football for another year, was held at the quarterback's family hunting camp. The camp, a modest cabin with no indoor plumbing or electricity, had kerosene lanterns swinging from the rafters dimly illuminating the kitchen and living area and the two bedrooms. The quarterback's dad had provided the keg of beer, leaving it on the kitchen counter to be found by the team.

In the grand small town tradition of Homecoming game nights, thirty-some kids drove to the camp after the game, planning to party with their friends before crashing at the cabin or driving themselves home.

The wide receiver and the quarterback rode together in the quarterback's car, an Oldsmobile Delta 88, nearly too wide to fit down the camp road, brushing the tree branches on both sides along the way. The wide receiver's sister followed in their family car. The three kids didn't have their driver's licenses yet, but again in the grand tradition of small towns, local law enforcement overlooked this as long as the kids drove responsibly and observed traffic laws.

The party commenced, music blaring from the camp radio, a fledgling bonfire in the fire circle battling the rain, muddy tracks decorating the plywood floors as kids ran to the fire and the outhouse.

The quarterback signaled the wide receiver's sister to follow him to the bedroom.

"I haven't talked to you all week," said the quarterback.

"I know, I've been so busy with tests and a research

paper I haven't really talked to anyone all week," replied the girl.

"I missed you."

"I missed you, too. I can't stop thinking about last weekend. When you pulled over and we danced on the car roof, I felt like we were the only two people in the world."

"We were the only two people in the world. In my world, anyway."

"Oh Howard, what are we going to do? I haven't told Mitch about us yet but he's going to figure it out. You know we don't keep secrets from each other and if he figures it out before I tell him, he's going to be really upset."

"I know, I don't like keeping this from Mitch either, but there hasn't been anything to tell him yet," an expression of hurt flashed across the girl's face. He continued, "I mean, until tonight. After tonight, if you feel the same way I do, then it's time to tell your brother about us."

The girl nodded, moving into the boy's embrace and returning his kiss as boldly as she dared. "Let's make out," she whispered.

"Ooh, the cheerleader is signaling the quarterback,"

he whispered back, pulling her down onto the bed. "And the quarterback is responding," he said, pushing her hand down until she felt a hard ridge in his jeans.

She quickly moved her hand back up to his chest, her other hand stroking the back of his head and neck, but he moved her hand back down.

The third time she moved her hand he let out a frustrated sigh. "What's the matter?"

"Nothing, I just don't want to do anything crazy. I just want to make out," she wiped her mouth.

"Well I'm not here to 'just make out' tonight. It's Homecoming, for Chrissakes, and so far this night has been perfect," he stroked her face lightly. "You don't want to ruin a perfect night, now, do you?"

"I don't think it would ruin a perfect night to make out with my new boyfriend and then tell my brother about it. How is that ruining a night?"

"Well, it's just that it would be so much more perfect if we could…go all the way." He stroked her cheek.

"I'm not ready for that. If that's what you're looking for, you've got the wrong girl."

"Oh come on, now. What could possibly go wrong? Are you scared?"

"No, I'm not scared. I'm just not ready," she stood up, straightening her clothes. "I'm sorry, Howard. No harm, no foul. I'll just get back to the party."

"Oh, no, you don't," he grabbed her arm, pinching her wrist between his thumb and finger.

"Ouch! Howard, knock it off. Look, we can both just forget about this and move on. It's no big deal."

"It's a big deal to me," he grinned, gesturing toward his crotch. "It's quite a large deal, actually, and we need to take care of it."

"Don't be silly, Howard." He squeezed her wrist harder. "Howard, you're scaring me. I'm going to call Mitch in here if you don't knock it off."

"Call all you want, he won't hear you. The radio is blasting and the party's so loud no one will hear anything."

He pushed her down and held her with one hand, groping for her zipper with the other. "If you're not going to let me, I'll just have to see what I can do," he said through clenched teeth.

Marcia, trapped now beneath Howard as he straddled her thighs, felt panic invading her chest as she gulped air. She flailed her arms in a pathetic attempt to pummel Howard, screaming "HOWARD! YOU STOP

IT RIGHT NOW!", kicking and punching without aim.

But Howard seemed to have entered another dimension, ignoring Marcia's pleas and ineffective thrashing and calmly proceeding to shuck her jeans down. He pinned her down with one arm across her upper chest, his face at once familiar and terrifying. The radio blared Sweet's new song, Ballroom Blitz, screeching a panicky serenade, matching Marcia's hysteria as Howard entered her. She'd never noticed before, incorrectly identifying the singer's tone as excitement and energy, but now she realized the singer was having an anxiety attack. His tone was an audio interpretation of her lurching stomach, her screaming nerves. Marcia channeled her thoughts and energy into the song and let it carry her away, mentally removing herself from her physical body. She had no idea whether a few minutes or an hour had passed; time seemed to step aside while she retreated into a numb state and maintained a formless, marginal awareness of herself. She focused on the ceiling to remove Howard's face from her field of vision. Her body remained rigid and she was aware of a distant rhythmical pounding, a rude invasion, a loss. An irreversible loss.

The thought of loss newly invigorated Marcia and she started flailing again, kicking and screaming, clawing at Howard's face and pulling his hair. His eerily robotic expression at once terrified and energized her. This couldn't be the Howard she knew; who was this monster ramming her, staring as if he didn't recognize her?

By the time the song's final chant started (*It's, it's a ballroom blitz; it's, it's a ballroom blitz*) Howard was re-zipped and asking what her trouble was, his voice oddly disconnected.

"You better thaw out if you ever want a husband," he stared down at her. "If I wanted Eskimo pie I'd goddamn well go buy one." He laughed at his own joke and stormed from the room.

Marcia finally realized she was still half-naked, her pain revealing itself in minute increments, a bruise on her right knee, a scratch on her face, blood on the quilt. The blood was somehow humiliating and accusatory and she felt vaguely guilty for allowing this evidence to record the ugly event.

She shivered, hauling herself up to get dressed, when Mitch burst into the room and surveyed the scene with one glance, taking in the rumpled quilt, the blood, and Marcia buttoning her jeans. His eyes found her stunned face and she watched the anger crawl across his face as he added all the details together before gathering her in for a comforting bear hug.

"Mitch," she whimpered.

"Ssh, no need to talk, Marsh," he stroked her hair. "No need to talk. I'm here." His feet started moving even as he told her this, his usual rasp deepening into a growl. He hugged her hard, then held her out so he could look into her eyes. "Will you be okay in here? I have to go take care of Howard."

She nodded, eyes large and watery. "I'll be fine," she whispered.

Mitch lowered her down to the bed, afraid she'd stumble and fall if he didn't guide her down safely. "I'll be back—stay put and wait for me," he called over his shoulder as he left the room and re-entered the party.

Marcia curled up on the bed, wrapping the quilt around her shoulders to stop shivering. Her teeth chattered, making her worry about choking on the vomit she fought to contain.

A quick glance around the living room and kitchen confirmed Mitch's suspicions: Howdy had already fled the cabin, probably planning to deny everything if questioned.

"Whatcha doin', Mitch? You look red, man," Bobby McKay, a linebacker healing from a broken shin, carried his crutches in one hand and his beer in the other, hopping unsteadily and plowing into Mitch. He regained his balance, his face two inches from Mitch's. "This is a party, man," he breathed hotly in Mitch's ear. "You're red and you're supposed to be cool. Cool as the breeze." He nearly collapsed in giggles while Mitch took his crutches and guided him to the couch, shooing a couple cheerleaders out of the way.

"Here, Bobs, let's get you situated over here," said Mitch.

"Injury trumps female," mumbled Bobby as he settled into the corner. "Thanks, Mitch, now I can watch the cheerleaders from here. This is a much better view." He winked at Mitch.

"Call me if you need anything," said Mitch, tossing him another beer. "This oughta hold you for a while," he grinned as gamely as possible at Bobby and sauntered out into the night, hoping he appeared in no particular hurry.

Once he escaped the cabin he breathed deep, taking in the night air. The rain, reduced to a light mist, refreshed and sharpened his mind. After fifteen seconds of contemplation he knew where to look for Howard.

Howard's car was closer than Mitch had anticipated: he was stuck in the mouth of the driveway in a mud hole that stretched across the entire lane. Without a healthy running start, most cars wouldn't make it through. Howard had tried to leave the party without his lights on, which demanded a slower pace and had caused him to spin ineffectively for twenty minutes, his tires spewing impressive clumps of wet, sticky mud on the trees behind him.

Mitch knocked on the driver's window. "Need a push?" he asked.

Howard nodded, gulped.

Mitch pretended not to notice. "We need more beer. I'll push you out and we can drive to town."

"Okay," squeaked Howard.

Mitch pushed, his shoulder to the rear bumper of Howard's Oldsmobile. It felt good to dispel some of his anger-fueled energy. He'd never felt this keyed up and ready for combat, not even before a football game. His hands itched to punch something; he used his whole body to push on Howard's car, starting from a crouch and ending up walking slowly while maintaining pressure on the trunk, until he reached the other end of the bowled-out mud hole.

He banged on the trunk and ran around to the driver's side, shoving Howard over as he took the wheel.

"What the hell?! This is my car, asshole," said Howard.

"I know, Howdy, but you're too drunk to drive right now. I've only had one beer so I'm driving. Move your ass over."

Howard slid to the passenger seat and stared out the window, sullen and gloomy.

"Okay," he whined.

"So, what was going on with you and Marcia back there?" Mitch squinted into the headlights' beams, peering through the gauze of rain.

Howard's eyes grew round. "Nothin', buddy. Why, what'd she say?"

Mitch let the radio static and the pounding rain fill the silence for a moment, allowing Howard's anxiety to ratchet up a notch. "She didn't say a word. I just wondered if something happened."

"You two and your goddamn twin non-talk," Howard sighed. "Alright, fine, something happened, okay? Your sister is a goddamned nun, as in 'don't want none'." He chuckled once, cruelly. "She's a fuckin' Eskimo pie. Cold as ice." He slumped down in the seat.

Mitch gripped the wheel and hit the brakes, suddenly realizing he'd passed the narrow lane he'd been watching for. He threw the car into reverse and backed up about thirty feet, not saying a word or looking at Howard.

"Where we goin', Mitch?" Howard sounded panicked.

"Oh, we're just going to take care of this situation," Mitch spoke clearly, almost comfortingly. He shifted into drive and turned onto another two-track lane, this one running three-quarters of the way around Bicycle Swamp before petering out in a large sandy area where they picked blueberries every August.

"Whaddaya mean?"

Mitch accelerated, careening along the sandy lane until they reached the first wide area. He killed the lights and shut off the car.

"Howard, we need to clear the air. You can't treat my sister like one of your whores or whatever you call them. She's my *sister* for Christ's sake," he glanced at his hands, wondering at the way they shook, fairly itching to punch something.

"Well then, buddy, let's go," said Howard, opening his door with resignation.

Mitch met him outside, having exited the driver's side and darted around the rear of the car. This was the first moment Howard realized he might have crossed a line with no bridge back to the other side.

"Oh, shit," said Howard, just as Mitch's first upper cut caught his left jaw, knocking it sideways. He sucker punched Mitch before Mitch landed another one on his nose.

Mitch's advantages, longer arms and a sober countenance, not to mention the pure rage fueling his entire body, quickly proved to Howard he was outfought.

"C'mon, Mitchie, let's not ruin our friendship," Howard started pleading. "I won't do it again, I promise."

"You can't undo it, Howd."

"Well, it's just that she seemed so, you know, hot and ready, almost begging for it, and suddenly she just shut it right the fuck off." He shook his head. "I don't know, I mean, I never thought any sister of yours would be such a crazy bitch."

Mitch heard some of what Howard said; the rage absorbed most of the sound. He knew, though, he didn't hear any regret or remorse in Howard's tone.

Howard didn't see Mitch's foot as he tripped Howard over backwards into the swamp, then jumped on top of him and wrapped his hands around Howard's throat. Years of playing football had strengthened his fingers, already longer than average thanks to genetics, and he easily reached around Howard's neck. It felt satisfying, holding Howard's entire neck in his hands, clamping his fingers tighter and ever tighter, plunging Howard's head down into the bog.

Both boys were drenched in swamp water. Howard felt stumps and logs beneath his back, creating a random pattern of bruises and contusions. His face turned a deep scarlet, his eyes bugging out as he fought for breath and gripped Mitch's wrists, hoping to pry them away from his neck. Howard managed a jagged breath just as Mitch pushed him under water again. Snot and vomit decorated the lower half of Howard's face.

Mitch, oddly removed from his actions, studied his hands around Howard's neck, watching his thumbs clamp tighter and lacing his fingers for a more secure grip. They stayed locked this way, Howard restricted by Mitch's powerful legs and hands, Mitch afraid to loosen and give Howard an opportunity to turn things around, until Howard stopped struggling.

Mitch noticed it first in Howard's body as it relaxed beneath him. He realized Howard was no longer pulling on his hands, trying to remove them from Howard's neck. Mitch watched Howard's face as he slackened his hold. Howard sank below the surface of the dirty bog water, slowly and casually, as if he was finally lying down for a much needed rest. Mitch crawled away from Howard and vomited until he lay weak and shaking in the weeds, gulping air and wondering where the strange, high humming sound was coming from. When it escalated into a scream he realized it was coming from his own throat.

Author Interview

How did you come up with the storyline for Superior Sacrifices?

One day, I was riding along with my husband in his pick-up truck while he went bird hunting. We went down our usual trails, and then tried one new trail, which lead us through a swamp. All of a sudden, the murder scene entered my head (spoiler alert—stop reading now if you don't want to know what happens), and I envisioned one boy choking another one, and holding his head under the brackish water until he stops breathing. Somehow, I knew the murderer was the good guy, so I went through my usual line of inner questioning:

Why did one boy murder the other? As revenge… for…something the other boy did to the first boy's sister. Immediately, I knew the victim had just date raped the murderer's sister. After a Homecoming game. On a rainy night. I could see the entire scene in my mind.

The questions kept coming, and I always had a ready answer. This all occurred in my mind, so my husband, three feet away, had no idea.

What happened to the sister? She got pregnant, of course.

What were their names? Mitch and Marcia. They're twins. Ooh! And the murder victim was Howard, Mitch's best friend.

What happened to Mitch? There's more than one town in the Upper Peninsula that boasts a zero murder conviction rate, so I knew this scenario would fit well into the category of homicide deaths that forever remain unsolved. *Superior Sacrifices* illuminates a dark corner of UP culture that people who don't live here never know exists.

Before we drove back to the main road, the entire storyline was mapped out and the characters had taken up residence in my head.

My husband turned to me and said, "what are you thinking about?"

"I think I'm going to write a book about twins," I said.

How did you arrive at the title Superior Sacrifices?

This work wasn't titled until a couple of months after I finished the manuscript. One morning, over coffee at a campground, my sister and I brainstormed until we came up with this title.

It's a perfect title, using the double entendre of Superior (the Lake, and the synonym for higher) and the word sacrifices, which works into the story nicely. Each character makes some sacrifice, large or small, during the story. The alliteration was a bonus.

The cover art is a photograph taken along a Lake Superior shoreline.

Is there really a town called Iron Falls?

Not in the UP. I didn't want to write a story about date rape and murder in my own town—we don't need bad karma around here!

I located Iron Falls farther west in the UP, so it was more heavily influenced by its proximity to Lake Superior.

Lake Superior is an awesome sight to behold—if you've never witnessed it on a calm day and a stormy day, you're missing out. The lake heavily influences our local weather, culture, and activities.

How was Superior Sacrifices received by your local town?

Very well. People tend to call it a mystery, but it isn't really a mystery because the reader knows who the murderer is immediately. It is a story of rape and murder, two rather dark subjects with which I have no first-hand experience. But it also showcases the special bond between twins—the almost telepathic form of communication twins use—and the special bond between townspeople in a small town in a geographically isolated area.

The UP is a unique culture, and one of my goals with this work was to capture one facet of that culture.

What does your writing routine look like?

I wish I had a writing routine! My writing is a well into which I dive, and I live there for weeks or months while the floors go unvacuumed and the counters unwiped. Then I'll resurface and resume my other hobbies for awhile, abandoning the writing until it calls me again.

I've tried several times to establish a writing practice with a measurable daily or weekly output, but I can only sustain that for a few months.

When I'm working on a book project I try to write every day, at least during the first draft phase. It's important to maintain close contact so I don't lose momentum.

About the Author

Jan Stafford Kellis lives in the wild woods of Michigan's Upper Peninsula. When she's not reading, writing, or luxury camping, she's running her handcrafted soap business, DeTour Soap Company. She visits Lake Superior as often as possible.

Visit www.jankellis.com for updates.

Other Books by Jan Stafford Kellis

Bookworms Anonymous:
A Non-Traditional Book Club for All Readers

Part memoir, part cookbook, and part informational
guide, this is an exclusive peek inside the closed society of
Bookworms Anonymous, a non-traditional book club in
De Tour Village, located in Michigan's Upper Peninsula.
This book takes the reader to eight book club meetings
(they're *never* called parties) and includes book reviews,
book handling commandments, recipes, and a guide for
beginning your own chapter of Bookworms Anonymous.

Bookworms Anonymous:
Volume II

The women are gathered again! Bookworms Anonymous
is a non-traditional reading group established in 2000,
comprised of seven women in Michigan's Upper
Peninsula. They meet monthly to share a gourmet
vegetarian meal and discuss and swap books. Part

memoir, part cookbook and part celebration of words and reading, Bookworms Anonymous Volume II contains many of the same things found in Volume I: reading group meetings, anecdotes, book reviews and recipes.

"A delightful read for any book lover, Bookworms Anonymous II is packed with great reading recommendations and insightful conversation from seven savvy readers. Book club-friendly recipes are a delicious bonus! Now, I'm off to the bookstore…"
- Kathleen Flinn, author of *The Sharper Your Knife, the Less You Cry* and *The Kitchen Counter Cooking School*

"A warm celebration of two of life's most vital ingredients--books and friendships."
- Ellen Airgood, author of *South of Superior* and *Prairie Evers*

"A love letter to reading, beautifully rendered, and with all the warmth and fun and closeness of your favorite book club on that perfect meeting night."
- Robert Kurson, author of *Shadow Divers* and *Crashing Through*

The Word That You Heard

Enid Forrester hates her name and her hair. On the first
day of summer in 1980 she can almost see the
wonderfully empty expanse of time stretching before her.
Enid comes of age in Michigan's Upper Peninsula, where
there isn't much to do in the summer or any other time
of year for a twelve-year-old girl. Her summer education
includes listening to the "drunken pontificators" lecture
in the coffee shop about what not to do as she joins her
dad at the local table for their morning refueling. Enid
learns life can't be distilled into mere words and small
towns sometimes offer the widest view of humanity.

A Pocketful of Light

Italy has it all and she's willing to share. Explore the
world's original tourist destination through this true story
told like a novel. The book features the Fibonacci
Sequence, a few non-painful history lessons and some
funky Italian phrases as well as the friendly recounting of
two travelers exploring the second greatest country in the
world.

The Sunshine Room

Ellen and her daughter Althea share an apartment in
Chicago. A Universe of two, they live a simple life and
take care of each other. When Ellen receives a call urging
her to her estranged father's hospital bedside, Ellen
wonders whether or not she should respond.

Is Ellen ready to face her own past, and subject Althea to
the long-held secrets she left behind?

Will Althea embark on her own journey to discover the
past she didn't know she had?

All books are available in fine book stores and online..
For the latest updates, or to book an appearance, please visit
www.jankellis.com.

Excerpt:

The Sunshine Room

Jan Stafford Kellis

Elle: March 31, 2008

They say there are three sides to every story: his, hers, and the truth. In my case, there were four sides: his, hers, mine, and the truth.

Like most stories, it began before we knew we were acting out events worth retelling. Well. Some of us may have known.

As far back as I can remember, I wanted a do-over. I daydreamed about it, obsessed about it, watched and re-watched *Back To The Future* and wished I had a DeLorean and access to plutonium.

A do-over would have given me the option to really invent myself, to fulfill my greatest potential. Who knows what I could have been: a lawyer, an architect, an engineer. I could have influenced the world.

January 5, 1985

She'd been up for hours wandering the house, making coffee and drinking too much of it. The moon, she was certain, was to blame for her restlessness. The knock on the door startled her. She tugged on the belt of her ancient terrycloth robe and approached the door.

She peered through the dusty window next to the door but it only afforded a view of the top of a down-turned head. Something familiar about it. A thin thread of foreboding uncoiled in her stomach and threatened to choke her. *How had he found her? Why hadn't he stopped searching?*

She considered running, sprinting out the back door, one child tucked under each arm, but she knew it was futile to attempt an escape. He'd found her here, in her safe haven. A place she hadn't known existed when she'd last seen him.

She opened the door.

"Sam." She pulled back and swallowed vomit before it spewed onto his shoes.

"I've missed you, sweetness." His sneer was terrifying —it signaled the beginning of a particularly brutal attack —but she remembered the best course of action was not to show her fear.

She shoved her hand into her robe and removed her wedding ring as she talked. "No, no. I thought you wanted me to leave. *Honest.* I left because I thought it was what *you* wanted."

"You never could lie, could you, Beth. In fact—"

He leaned close as if to nuzzle her neck, and she flinched back two steps.

"—I always considered your inability to lie one of your best character flaws."

"Lie, truth, whatever. I'm stating facts." She blinked, a caricature of honesty.

"Car's running." He jabbed a thumb over his shoulder toward the street.

More bile. She held up her hands, showed him double stop signs. "I can't leave."

"Pack. Your. Bags."

She shook her head. "No. I—"

"So we'll travel light." He grabbed her wrist.

"Okay, okay." *How to stall?* "Give me a few minutes." She'd run into the girls' room and grab her babies, then jump out the window and run as fast as she could. It was crazy, but no way she'd leave without her babies. What could she do? She had no choice. She knew she couldn't take the babies with her—Sam wouldn't hesitate to sell them off, and they'd be safe here. Their father could raise them. He'd do a good job.

"Go ahead. Try to escape again. I know you've got a couple of marketable little princesses in the other room, and I'm not opposed to selling them off to the highest bidder." He laughed cruelly. "Or the first bidder."

"You wouldn't!"

He spoke deliberately. "I would, and you know I would. Now pack your bags. Your little mister will figure things out. He'll get by without you, don't you worry about him. And if you get your perky little ass in gear in the next ten minutes, he won't have to know about your past." He smiled, an evil snake's smile with glassy eyes and pointy chin. "You haven't told him about your past, have you?"

"Well, I—"

"No, you haven't. Or he wouldn't have married you and given you two valuable babies."

"You stop it right now."

"I'll stop. If you pack. Your. Bags. I'm getting tired of waiting. *Beth.*"

She couldn't stomach the thought of her husband finding out about her past. She'd been so careful to cover her tracks. How had Sam found her hundreds of miles from where she'd left him?

She ran into the bedroom to pack her things. She threw on a pair of jeans and a shirt, then scrawled a note on the index card she'd been using as a bookmark. She shoved the note into her jewelry box, where it stuck in the lid. *Perfect.* She scrawled a second note, a decoy in case Sam came in here, and left it on the bed.

Beth crammed some clothes into a tote bag and ran back out to the entryway. He was gone. Then she heard a floorboard creak and realized he had walked down the hallway to the girls' room. She tiptoed after him.

"Sam!" She hissed.

"I don't know if I'd sell them." He whispered, nodding toward the darkened room. "They might be worth more to me alive, like their mother." He ran his dirty index finger along her jawline and she held still, knowing if she shuddered he'd punish her.

She grabbed his forearm and tugged him toward the front door, dreading starting over once again. She'd thought she was finished with starting over.

The car roared away, and the town returned to silence.

Elle: March 31, 2008

People often assumed I was a widow. I rarely corrected them.

I welcomed this assumption—some might say I encouraged it. I wore a wide gold band on my wedding ring finger, the kind of band that leaves no question in the observer's mind about what kind of ring it is. I also perfected my phrasing: *I'm a single mother now*, I'd say. Or, *It's just Althea and me now.* Or my favorite, *Life isn't easy without Althea's dad.*

All of these statements were true. It wasn't my fault, or my problem, if people assumed that I'd once had a husband, and he had since died. When anyone asked me directly if I'd ever been married, I answered truthfully.

It was the easiest way I'd found to send a clear signal of unavailability, without wearing an actual sign.

I hated meeting new people—especially men. I blamed this on my small-town upbringing, where we rarely encountered anyone we hadn't known since conception.

What I despised was the initial small talk, the here's-my-life-story, do-you-still-like-me dance. You might think this odd for someone who ran a hotel and met countless guests every week, but that was merely surface-meeting. No dance required.

Whenever well-meaning people asked me where I was from and what brought me to Chicago, I lost all balletic conversational coordination. My answers spilled out in clumsy discord while my potential friend shifted on his feet and stared at the far wall, wishing himself away. I would then pirouette and escape to the safety of the ficus in the corner. The ficus understood.

Feeling like an awkward slow-motion hand-jive performer with a dismal sense of social rhythm, I preferred standing alone in a crowd to standing in a group dodging stilted conversational overtures. Insincerity caused me indigestion.

Strangers sensed my foundering like dogs sensed fear. Somehow, these people already knew I had failed to meet expectations. And so the interrogation would begin.

***

Every time I saw a prematurely gray man—think circa-1980 Steve Martin, with less-jolly eyes—I was slammed back into my fifteen-year-old self, defensive and anxious and uber-insecure. My pre-Chicago self. The self I was before I'd left a place where everyone else knew your story better than you did.

But today wasn't going to be one of those days. Today my feet — and mind—would remain firmly in the present. Today was Althea's thirteenth birthday, and I told myself I wouldn't work late again, but I knew I couldn't alter reality. I'd already missed so many milestones in her life, I deserved an entry in the Guinness Book of World Records. What would my title be: World's Workingest Mom?

Her birthday gifts were wrapped and ready, all but one of them stashed under my desk.

I'd planned to leave work early today and surprise Althea, but the semi-annual sales convention week meant longer hours for everyone at the Phoenix Hotel.

I turned the lobby music down a notch, humming along to *Call Me Al* while I waited for the last salesman to finish his phone conversation and let me check him into his room. I'd spent the day covering for Adam, our newest employee, who had called in sick with mono. I liked filling in occasionally, but not at the expense of Althea's birthday.

This I knew for sure: salespeople were too ebullient and way too helpful. If I ran around wasting my energy grinning at everyone and rushing to hold doors for people and helping strangers carry their luggage, all while appearing primped and pressed and ready to hold an audience with the President, I'd collapse. Maybe salespeople were made of sturdier material than the average human.

Although, the superhuman salespeople generally only engaged in surface-meeting. I bet they each had their secrets, carefully guarded behind casual, manufactured answers to polite social questions.

I suppose I, too, was a kind of salesperson, but I was the quiet kind, the kind who respected personal boundaries and relaxed her face once in a while.

The man (Steve Martin's younger brother?) finally pocketed his phone and strode toward the counter, piercing salesman gaze and crisp collar, perfect teeth displayed in a symmetrical smile.

"How's my favorite receptionist today?" His hair was more black than gray, but his facial stubble was all silver.

I couldn't tell if he was trying to grow a beard, or if he was a lazy shaver. Maybe he was going for the magazine-cover look: affected rugged sophistication.

"Happy and busy, as usual," I said. I smiled to soften my tone. "Name?"

His face rearranged itself into a mock frown. "You don't remember my name? I'm crushed." He slumped his shoulders, defining a wiry frame beneath his suit jacket. "It's only been six months since I stayed here last. We had a drink in the hotel bar." He straightened back to his ramrod posture and snapped his fingers, turning the light back on in his hazel eyes.

I noticed they were jollier than I'd first thought.

"You ordered…a whiskey sour, and I told you that was an old person's drink, and you should try a cosmo." He winked.

He actually winked! Could anyone be more arrogant? The cute ones were always arrogant. My stomach fluttered. "I'm sorry, Mr. Jamison—"

"Aha! You *do* remember my name!" He held up one index finger—a personal mini-victory. "I knew I must have made *some* impression on you."

I half-smiled at him, allowing him this scant point. The clock in the lower right corner of the computer screen read 6:00 p.m. Birthday party time. *Where was Mindy?* I wondered. She was scheduled for the six o'clock shift, but she operated within her own time zone. I looked at Joel, then slowly inhaled and exhaled. *Must tamp down impatience.* "Well, you're the last one to check in, so yours is the only name left on my screen. As I was saying, I'm sorry, but I meet so many people here, it's impossible to remem—"

"Oh, but you remember me. We had that drink. We talked. You have a daughter, named…Alyssa? No. Alison?"

I printed out his room reservation sheet and placed it on the counter for him to initial and sign. He stared at the ceiling, palms on the counter. His fingers were long and tapered, the nails trimmed short, no callouses or scars from manual labor. My hands, small though they were, probably looked more workworn than his did.

"Al….Al…Althea!" He snapped his fingers again, pointing at me. "I knew I'd remember it! My ability to recall details is what sets me apart, you know. It's the best skill to have when you're in my business. If you'd like, I could help you develop a system so you can easily recall details about your customers, too. It makes people feel special, when you remember their names." He was in full sales mode. "And by the way, you can call me Joel." He pointed upward, circling his finger to indicate the sound system. "*Call Me Al.* Good song choice."

"Thank you, Joel. I'm—"

"Elle. You're Elle. I remember," he said quietly. He looked at me for two full seconds, then tapped his temple. "Details. They're all in here, cataloged and indexed and ready to retrieve. You're still wearing your decoy wedding ring." He nodded toward my hand.

There was a tiny scar above one eye, a diagonal line through his eyebrow.

"Why mess with something that works?" We looked at each other for a few seconds, and I considered removing my ring right then, but what kind of signal would that send? I might as well wrap my legs around him and ask him to carry me to his room.

I spied Mindy entering the Hotel, a few minutes late for her shift, but early enough to break the spell. "I am leaving--right now." I nodded a greeting at Mindy as she walked across the lobby and through the Employees Only door to stand behind the counter with me. "It's my daughter's birthday and we're having a couple of people over for dinner." Why was I telling him more personal information? I knew he'd just spew it back at me the next time we had a conversation, and he'd probably want a pat on the head for his performance.

"I'm sorry I'm late!" Today, Mindy's hair was black tipped in brilliant pink. "I thought I was relieving Adam." She tugged her sleeves down to her wrists to hide her tattoos.

"He's sick with mono. I'm not sure how long he'll be out." I gestured toward the computer and the stack of files. "I'll finish this last check-in, and then I've gotta run. You should have a pretty quiet night."

Joel glanced at his phone, every gesture a delay. "March thirty-first. Althea's birthday. Got it. Is she turning thirteen?"

Why was it so annoying to me that he tracked these details? And why couldn't he do it on his own time? All my life, at least the portion of it I'd lived on my own, no one had paid me this much intense attention.

I wondered if he cheated on his wife. I didn't see a wedding ring, but that's what cheaters did—removed their rings during sales conventions. How many men had I observed over the years with faint lines or dents where their wedding rings usually rode? Enough to qualify as cliche. Unmarked husbands. Joel Jamison probably never wore a wedding ring, to avoid the whole issue of camouflaging his dented finger.

"Yes, thirteen. You have a remarkable memory." I tapped his reservation form and spoke quickly. "You're in room 339. Do you need more than one key?"

"339. That's auspicious. One key will be fine." He grinned. "Unless you'd like one."

"That won't be necessary, Mr. Jamison."

"Kidding! I'm kidding. And please don't think I talk this way to every hotel receptionist. This is out of character for me. Want me to tell you an easy way to remember my room number?"

I didn't have time to correct him, to point out my Manager name tag and ask him why he assumed I was a receptionist. The clock thundered on, tick and tock. "Sure."

"Threes are always lucky, and anything divisible by three is lucky. My life tends to run on threes. But the easiest way to remember my room number is: three times three is nine. Three-three-nine." His hands shot out, palms up, to illustrate how simple it was.

"Thanks for the tip." I picked up a pile of files and half-turned away, hoping he'd take the hint. "Enjoy your stay."

"One more thing, Elle."

I turned back toward him, just a quarter turn, clutching the files.

"I know you're busy right now, but…are you free tomorrow evening? Maybe we could have dinner. Or something." The word 'beseeching' skated across my brain as I gazed at his face.

I wasn't prepared for this. Most salesmen flirted with me just enough to ensure I'd maintain discretion when I received a call from the person with a matching dent on their wedding ring finger. Of course, most salesmen didn't realize my own ring was a decoy.

"I'll have to check my calendar." What? Why hadn't I said no? I'd expected to hear myself say no, thank you, and have a good evening, but instead my treacherous mouth formed a vague answer with enough hope to keep him hanging. I smiled, but only after my face revealed my private horror.

"Okay, I'll check with you tomorrow. I'm here for four nights, as you know, so…do you like lasagne?"

His tone gentled, and his shoulders relaxed. His ring finger looked like it had never been inhabited.

"Si." I nodded.

"Has anyone ever told you that you look like Jennifer Aniston?"

"Well—"

"I mean, not exactly—but when you are partially turned away, there's something about your eyes and nose that resembles her. And your hair is the same color and style."

"Thank you. I've been told that a few times, but I can't see it."

"I'm sure it doesn't show up in the mirror—too close and centered. I'll try to capture it on a photo and show you." He grabbed his suitcase handle. "But not today. I've bothered you enough for today. Think about dinner, and let me know." He saluted and sauntered toward the elevator.

I stacked the files on my desk and retrieved Al's gifts and the helium balloon I'd bought earlier, wished Mindy a hasty good night, and ran out the door.

***

The balloon floated along, gentle tugs on the ribbon I clutched, while I speed-walked three blocks south, then two blocks west to our apartment building.

I wondered if anyone had yet invented balloon therapy. It's impossible to feel anything but happiness with a balloon bopping along above your head, even when you're running late. It's also impossible to run with a balloon bopping along above your head, because the mental image would make you collapse with hilarity.

My thoughts kept turning to Joel Jamison as I walked. I couldn't seem to reclaim my mind. I breathed deeply even as I scurried along the sidewalks, inhaling the calm quiet of our neighborhood, exhaling the relentless cheer of the salespeople. Every six months, I somehow forgot how exhausting it was during sales convention week. Although, if I wasn't running The Phoenix Hotel and trying to survive sales convention week, I wouldn't have met Joel. Not that I'd ever needed a man in my life. Fickle old things. It would be nice, though, to go out on a date once in a while. I think. I'd never been on a real date, but it looked fun on TV.

By the time I arrived at the door to our building, my thoughts circled so fast I'd worn myself out. I would tell Joel no. He did seem different from other men, and he was the least annoying of the salespeople who attended this semi-annual conference, but I had no vacancy in my life for the complications, commitments and compromises that came along with a relationship.

Our apartment door was unlocked, as it usually was at this time of day. Althea inhabited half of the building, constantly running up and down the stairs to Mrs. Whitcomb's and Malcolm's apartments. We were lucky to have such great neighbors—our own little village within these walls. I could hear Malcolm and Mrs. Whitcomb talking and laughing.

I flung the door wide and pushed the balloon into the room. "Happy birthday!"

Everyone turned toward me and started talking at once, greeting me and taking the gifts from my arms.

"Oh, my land, girl! You look like a walking birthday party!" said Mrs. Whitcomb.

"Mom. A balloon? Really? I'm thirteen." Althea smiled to soften her faux-snarky comments.

"Yes, you're aging by the second. Enjoy the balloon before the wrinkles start forming," I told her.

"I'm almost as old as you are!" Althea took the balloon and tied it to the wine bottle on the table.

"Fifteen years is fifteen years," said Malcolm. He squeezed my arm. "Salutations, Ms. Marchand."

"Good evening, Malcolm. The table looks great! Thank you for setting it. I'm so sorry I'm late."

"We all pitched in a little, dear. None of us has anyplace to go, so don't fret." Mrs. Whitcomb smiled. "Now have a seat here. I poured you a glass of wine." She pulled out my chair.

"Thank you. Wine sounds fabulous." I kicked off my shoes and removed my jacket before sinking into the chair. "I feel like it's *my* birthday—what a nice way to end the work day."

Malcolm and Mrs. Whitcomb settled into their chairs, one on each side of Althea.

"Did you have a long day, Mom?"

"Not bad—the sales convention people checked in today. Adam has mono. Typical Monday. Next week is the women's yoga retreat, so a vast improvement is on the horizon."

I sipped my wine and looked at Althea. She'd braided a section of hair and applied a pale pink lip gloss. She looked like an innocent twenty-year-old.

"How was your day, Al-Critter?"

"I had a great day! No one at school remembered that it's my birthday, Mrs. Whitcomb made me a great snack, Malcolm didn't have any new books to catalog. It's like I had a day off." She grinned. "I think being thirteen agrees with me."

"The secret to a happy life," said Malcolm, holding up his crooked index finger, "is to make sure every age agrees with you."

"That is so true! Oh, my land, I can tell you, seventy-eight agrees with me just fine. Although, I do sometimes wish I could be sixty-five again. That was a great year." Mrs. Whitcomb smiled and sipped her wine. The rhinestones on her glasses sparkled.

"Well, that was thirteen years ago!" Althea reached over and squeezed Mrs. Whitcomb's arm. "Of course it was a great year!"

We all chuckled.

"Now that we're all present, let's commence serving." Malcolm stood and scooped the stew out of the crock pot. He placed a slice of the French bread he'd brought alongside each bowl of stew. "Where are Roberta and young Courtney this evening?" he asked.

"They couldn't make it. Roberta's sister is having a family dinner." I'd met Roberta at work, when we cleaned rooms together for one summer season, and we'd been close ever since. Now she was a yoga teacher and counsellor, helping single mothers (many of them teens) find jobs and support themselves. Courtney was a year younger than Althea, and the girls had a strong friendship as well.

After dinner, I cleared the plates and placed a stack of gifts in front of the birthday girl. She tore into the first package, from Mrs. Whitcomb. A pair of knitting needles and yarn.

"The plain white yarn is for practicing, and the nice yarn is for your first real project." Mrs. Whitcomb said. "We can start lessons whenever you're ready."

"Thank you! I've been wanting to learn how to knit," said Althea. "I want to make a sweater."

Mrs. Whitcomb laughed. "You might want to start with a scarf, dearie. Or a hot pad."

Malcolm gave Althea a book, as always. "It's *Little Women!*" Althea said as she ripped open the paper. "My teacher talked about this book the other day, and she told us that Louisa May Alcott is one of her favorite authors. Maybe I'll write a book report on this, and get extra credit!" She looked at Malcolm, and I could see she loved him like a grandfather. "Thank you, Malcolm."

"My pleasure, my girl." He nodded and grinned, revealing his piano key teeth.

Al always saved my gifts for last. She tore through the paper and held up a black dress with cap sleeves, then

grabbed a pair of black pumps from the box and dangled
them so we could all see them. "Thank you, Mom! I love
it all."

"Keep digging," I told her. She found the play tickets
in the bottom of the box. "We're going to have a girls'
day," I said. "We'll go to the museum of your choice,
dinner downtown, and the play."

"*Chicago!*" she shouted. "I have tickets to *Chicago*.
We're going to see *Chicago* in Chicago. That is so cool."
She sounded breathless. "Thank you, Mom."

"Oh, my land, that play is a bit…gritty," said Mrs.
Whitcomb.

"It is." I nodded. "But I think Al is old enough now.
Like she said, she's almost as old as I am!"

Althea laughed and straightened her back.

"I've already read the play, anyway, and my friends
have seen it," she said.

"Children grow up fast these days," said Mrs.
Whitcomb.

"I have one more gift for you," I said. I ran into my
bedroom to retrieve the professionally wrapped package
from the closet, then ran back to the dining room and
held it out. "I splurged."

She unwrapped this one slowly. "Ooh, is this what I
think it is? Is it what I've been asking for?" Her hands
moved as she talked, fingers slipping under the tape,
prying the carefully folded layers apart. "The box is a little
bigger than I thought…Wow, Mom. A laptop? Are you
sure we can afford this?" She was still, looking at me with
an adult seriousness.

I hoped she wasn't disappointed to see a laptop instead of an iPhone.

"Yes, I've been saving for it. We have a pretty good nest egg, Al-Cheeks, so don't worry. However," I held up one finger, "I'm not yet ready to pay for Wi-Fi. You'll have to come to the hotel when you want to use the Internet."

"That's great! That will be great. I'll go to the hotel more often. Ooh! I'll be like those business people who are always staying there. So cool! Thank you so much!" She launched herself out of her chair to hug me.

"I know you wanted an iPhone," I told her. "But the monthly fees are too high. It's just not practical. I hope that's okay."

"It's fine." She tempered her disappointment with a smile. "I can still text Courtney from my laptop, when I'm on Wi-Fi." She lifted the computer over her head. "I have a MacBook! Yahoo! I'm going to bring it everywhere."

"How did you escape the technological revolution?" Malcolm asked me. "It seems everyone is perpetually focused on their electronic devices, and you don't even own one."

"Not a priority." I sipped my wine. "I wasn't even introduced to a computer until I worked at The Phoenix. I have a laptop, but only because I'm going to school and they required it."

"Mom's the only parent in my class who isn't on Facebook," said Althea. "And she's the youngest mom there is! Everyone else's mom is old and wrinkly."

Everyone laughed at this.

I glanced around the table at our ersatz family and thought, not for the first time, that family is made up of those you've chosen, rather than those you've acquired in a biological crap shoot.

The phone sounded like it always did, shrilling an alert with no ominous overtones.

"Hello?"

"Is this Ellen Marchand?" The voice was unfamiliar, pinched and proper.

I hadn't been called Ellen in years. The sound of my full name made me feel ten years old.

"Yes it is."

"Hello, Ellen. I'm calling about Jack Marchand. I understand you're his next-of-kin."

I sat down and listened. I wondered if I cared.

9 780999 103111